Diary of a Teenage Girl

Chloe Book N°. 2

SOLD OUT

a novel

MELODY CARLSON

Multnomah Publishers
Sisters, Oregon

SOLD OUT
published by Multnomah Publishers, Inc.
and in association with the literary agency of Sara A. Fortenberry

© 2003 by Melody Carlson

International Standard Book Number: 1-59052-141-2

Cover design by David Carlson Design
Cover image by Kwame Zikomo/Superstock

Scripture quotations are from:
The Holy Bible, New International Version © 1973, 1984 by International
Bible Society, used by permission of Zondervan Publishing House
The Holy Bible, King James Version

Multnomah is a trademark of Multnomah Publishers, Inc.,
and is registered in the U.S. Patent and Trademark Office.
The colophon is a trademark of Multnomah Publishers, Inc.

Printed in the United States of America

For information:
MULTNOMAH PUBLISHERS, INC.
POST OFFICE BOX 1720
SISTERS, OREGON 97759

Library of Congress Cataloging-in-Publication Data

Carlson, Melody.
    Sold out : a novel / by Melody Carlson.
       p. cm. -- (Diary of a teenage girl ; Chloe book 2)
Summary: Conflicts arise when fifteen-year-old Chloe Miller and her fellow band members
are discovered by a talent scout from Nashville and are invited to record and tour.
    ISBN 1-59052-141-2 (pbk. : alk. paper)
    [1. Bands (Music)--Fiction. 2. Chirstian life--Fiction.] I. Title.
    PZ7.C216637So 2003
    [Fic]--dc21

                                                              2003005467

03 04 05 06 07 08—10 9 8 7 6 5 4 3 2 1 0

What Readers Are Saying about
DIARY OF A TEENAGE GIRL SERIES...

My Name Is Chloe

"Readers will delight in this edgier, more intense, electric guitar-playing lead character."—*Publishers Weekly*

"*My Name Is Chloe* should be read by every teenager and makes a great crossover book or ministry tool."—*Christian Retailing*

On My Own

"i love all the books cause they relate to my life in some way or another."—ABBIE

Who I Am

"It's so refreshing to read about the life of a Christian girl for once. I can't get enough!"— JAMEY LYNNE

"This is such an amazing, inspirational book and i have gotten so much out of it."—AMALIE

"This was so cool!! It actually helped me w/my real life!! I even prayed some of the prayers that she wrote down!"—HEATHER

"Wonderful! Another perfect book to go along with the first two."—DANI

"I really enjoyed it. When I read it, it made me realize my commitment to God was fading. Since then I have become rejuvenated and more committed."—ERICA

It's My Life

"This book inspired me to persevere through all my hardships and struggles, but it also brought me to the reality that even through my flaws, God can make Himself known in a powerful, life-changing way."—MEGHAN

"This book is unbelievable... It's so absolutely real to any teenage girl who is going through the tribulations of how to follow God. I've just recently found my path to God, and I can relate to Caitlin in many ways—it's a powerful thing."—EMILY

"I loved it!! It was so inspirational and even convicted me to have a stronger relationship with Christ. Thanks, Melody, this is the series I've been waiting for!!!"—SARAH

Becoming Me

"As I read this book, I laughed, cried, and smiled right along with Caitlin. It inspired me to keep my own journal. It changed my life forever. Thank you."—RACHEL

"I love all of the books! I could read them over and over!!!"—ASHLEY

"I couldn't put it down. When I was finished, I couldn't wait to get the second one!"—BETHANY

One

Friday, April 11

Six months ago (to this very day!) I gave my life to God. And right now I feel like a complete failure. I can just see God shaking His head at me, thinking, "Get it together, girl!" Or maybe not—God is more mature than that, more gracious, more kind.

Yet who would've guessed that a day that started so well would go so crooked? Just goes to show you we don't have as much control over things as we'd like to believe. And even when we think we're doing everything right, it can still go wrong. Anyway, I got up early, spent some time with God, printed out copies of my latest song (for Allie and Laura to look over), and even rode my bike to school—part of my new "get fit" regime. I was feeling pretty good.

But now it seems I can't even do the simplest of things! I mean, how many times have I read Jesus' words—where He tells us to love, not just our friends, but everyone, even our enemies? <u>How many times</u>? And okay, I'll admit I still have a hard time loving my enemies. Take Tiffany Knight for instance. She's a pretty tough chick to love. Still, I ask for God's help on a regular basis, and I haven't done anything too lame lately. At least not to Tiffany.

Unfortunately, I blew it with one of my very best friends today, and I can't really blame her for being mad at me right now. Actually, I'm still pretty ticked at her too, but I know I was wrong, selfish, stupid even. Worst of all, I feel like crud to have been so incredibly immature in front of a bunch of our friends. How moronic is that? I'm not blind. I know that people watch me, Allie, and Laura to see how we act, how we treat others.

Ever since our band, Redemption, has been getting better known, it's as if we've suddenly turned into God's poster kids—like no mistake will go unnoticed. It probably sounds as if I'm becoming a bit paranoid, but I don't think so. I think they ARE watching, and waiting...for days just like today. And really, I'm not complaining about that so much, because it's what I wanted. I do want my friends to see my life for what it is—up close and personal—but hopefully so they can see God in me. Not me acting like a total jerk. That's why I'm infuriated at myself right now. I feel as though I made God look bad, and I hate when that happens.

It all started out in the cafeteria. Laura and Allie and I were eating together like we often do, although not always. Laura's friends LaDonna and Mercedes were sitting with us too, along with a few others, and we were all having a pretty good time until Laura pulled out a copy of my latest song, the one I'd given her just this morning. I'd hoped we could pull it together to perform next month at the All God's Children festival. And this is especially important to me because the money we make there will go to such a great cause.

But anyway, it became quite obvious that Laura didn't like my song. And now that I think about it, she seemed to be in a fairly obnoxious mood today. She'd already yipped at LaDonna about something or other and had been complaining about lunch (although that's understandable).

"This stanza is <u>so</u> cliché." Her voice seemed to take on that somewhat superior tone that she uses occasionally. But then I sort of understand how she's like that sometimes. I think it's her way of saying, "Hey, I'm important too."

"Cliché?" I leaned over to see which line she was referring to, at the same time telling myself to just chill, don't take offense. I mean, Laura has every right to her opinion.

"Yeah, it's just kind of boring."

"Boring?" Now that seemed a pretty strong opinion to me.

"Aw, it's not that bad," injected Allie before taking a bite of pizza.

Laura pressed her lips together. "Well, maybe

'boring' is the wrong word. But I guess the words fall kind of flat on me."

"Flat?" I'm sure my voice sounded a little flat at this point. I was starting to think it might've been nice if Laura had saved her criticism until later—a more private time when not so many ears were tuned in. I suppose this means I still have a problem with my pride. I glanced around the group and pretended not to care what they or anyone else thought, but I could see they were pretty amused by our little conflict. I shrugged. "Well, if you really don't like it—"

"It's not that I don't like the <u>whole</u> song. But this verse right here feels so cliché."

"Yeah, you mentioned that." It's possible I snapped those words out.

"You don't have to get so offended, Chloe."

"I'm not." I folded my arms across my chest and desperately tried to act nonchalant. "But you don't have to be so critical, either."

"Sorry." I could hear the irritation intensifying her voice. "I didn't know you had such thin skin."

"Well, think about it, Laura. No writer likes being told she's 'cliché.'"

"Fine. I guess I should've just told you that I'm sure I've heard this line in about a dozen other songs."

"<u>What</u> songs?" I realized my voice was increasing in volume now, but it seemed as if she was taking this whole thing way too far.

"Oh, lots of songs. I think it might've even been in an old Beatles song—"

"So you're saying the Beatles are cliché?"

She rolled her eyes at me. "No, I think you are cliché."

"Well, thanks a lot!" I snatched the paper from her hands and stood.

"Don't get mad, Chloe." This came from Allie. And no defense of my lyrics either; she seemed to assume this was just my problem.

"I'm not mad." I picked up my tray. "I think I need a change of scenery is all." And then I walked over to where Allie and I used to always eat, but now only eat sometimes. Today Jake, Cesar, Spencer, and a new girl named Marissa were sitting there.

"Hey, Chloe," called Cesar. "I thought maybe you'd ditched us for good."

I set down my tray. "Nah. It's just that we've been using lunchtime to work on some things for the next concert." Okay, that was partially true, but not completely. And I guess they saw through me.

Especially Jake. He looked unconvinced. "Aw, don't give us that bull, Chloe. We all know that Laura thinks she's too good for us. I used to think she was kinda cool, but now I think she's just like the rest of them." He glanced back to the table I'd just abandoned. "Even now she's looking over here like we're some nasty, trashy influence on you." He made a face imitating her.

I had to laugh. "No, that's not it. The reason she's scowling like that is because we just had a little spat."

"What about?" asked Marissa with obvious curiosity. "I thought you Christian kids always got along with each other."

Now I wished I'd kept my mouth shut. "Oh, it was nothing. She just didn't like a song I'd written."

Spencer laughed. "Oh yeah, I get it. Can't take the criticism, can you? Sure, it's fun when everyone's clapping and thinking you're great—"

"Man, are you in the wrong biz if you can't take the heat," added Cesar. "You ever read music reviews? Those critics can be pretty cruel, you know."

"I know and I would expect that kind of crud from a music critic. But it seems like your own band should be a little more understanding and supportive."

Marissa patted my shoulder in what seemed a somewhat demeaning way. "You're absolutely right, Chloe. And if I was in your band, I'd never pick on you."

I rolled my eyes. "Thanks, I feel so much better now."

"Yeah, too bad Marissa can't carry a tune,"

added Cesar. "You could throw Laura out and sign her up."

"Thanks, <u>Julius</u>." Marissa tossed him a look. She liked to call him "Julius" to aggravate him—like for Julius Caesar (pronounced see-sir, when Cesar's name is actually pronounced say-zar).

Anyway, hoping to change the subject, I turned my attention to Marissa. "So, are you feeling better about your move now?" I asked. The last time she and I had spoken, she was still feeling depressed about changing schools in the middle of the year.

"I guess." She glanced around the table and smiled halfheartedly. "These guys are treating me pretty good."

Spencer stood. "Yeah, but she still won't go out with any of us." He nodded to Jake. "Wanna get some fresh air?"

I shook my head. "Man, you really need a new line, Spencer. That one's getting pretty frazzled, you know."

"Yeah," Marissa chimed in with a twinkle in her eye. "Why don't you just admit that you're going out behind the school to puff on some weed?"

Spencer glared at her, then let loose with some profanity before he scuffled away, trying, I'm sure, to act cool. I have to admit that his language bothers me more than it used to, but I also remind myself that it's just where he's at right now. And I believe Jesus wants me to accept him—as he is.

I turned my attention back to Marissa. Now I need to point out that she's a really interesting looking girl—quite pretty actually, although I suspect she doesn't have a clue. She has this gorgeous long dark hair and startling green eyes that she outlines heavily in black. Today she had on a short denim skirt and tall boots. "So how come you won't go out with any of these guys?" I asked.

She glanced at Cesar. "Just not with the ones who've asked."

So then I realized, with a slight jolt, that she's after him. But what's that to me? I'd already made it perfectly clear I wasn't interested in getting involved with Cesar right now anyway. Yet I did experience a teeny twinge of jealousy just then. Naturally I tried to conceal this with another question. "So what do you do for fun then?"

She shrugged. "Not much."

"You want to do something with Allie Curtis and me this weekend?"

Her eyes lit up. "Sure."

"Let me see what's up with Allie and then give you a call."

"Cool."

The bell started to ring and I picked up my tray. "Later," I said as I headed out. At the tray drop-off I saw Laura, and she had on a scowl that looked to be carved right into her forehead. "You didn't have to get into a huff like that, Chloe, just because you didn't like my opinion."

I shrugged as I dumped my tray. I suppose I still felt hurt, or maybe just sorry for myself. I know I wanted her to apologize to me first. And I'm sure if she'd shown the slightest degree of sympathy, the whole thing would've blown over right then and there. And I'd have apologized to her too. For sure. So why didn't we just resolve the whole stupid thing right then and there? Why go to the trouble to bear grudges when it only makes you feel horrible?

She nodded over to where Marissa and Cesar were just leaving the table. "Chloe, do you really think you should be hanging with those guys?"

"_Those_ guys?" Okay, maybe I was just mad, but something about her tone ignited something in me. I suppose it was indignation. And I narrowed my eyes at her. "What exactly do you mean by that?"

"I just happen to think it's wrong, is all."

Well, this is when I lost it. I mean, it's not the first time Laura has pulled this, and today it just got to me. "What is with you, Laura?" I asked loudly (stupidly drawing even more attention).

"Why are you so down on absolutely everyone and everything? What kind of Christian are you supposed to be anyway?"

Her eyes flashed at me, but she said nothing, just turned away.

"Fine!" I shouted after her. "Be that way!"

"Time to lighten up," said Allie quietly, coming up from behind and placing her hand on my shoulder. "Chill."

"Why?" I demanded. "Why do I need to chill when Laura goes around acting like she's God's special appointee to judge everyone?"

"I think she's having a bad day."

"I'll say!"

And so Laura and I didn't speak to each other again for the remainder of the day. And now I feel rotten about it. I don't know why I couldn't just keep my big mouth shut. But part of what I said is true. I don't know why she has to act so judgmental and critical sometimes. And in her defense she's not <u>always</u> like that. But I also realize her church is fairly conservative and that has to affect her somewhat. But, honestly, sometimes I just wish she would <u>lighten up</u>.

JUDGING NOT

God, what do You think
when we make a stink?
should people go 'round

always putting down
look down their noses
as another mind closes?
God, why can't we be
more open and free?
hey, didn't You teach
how it is we'll reach
other ones for You
if we can be true
to the way You live
and how You forgive
with a perfect love
poured from above?
please, help me, i pray
show me Your way
cm

Two

Saturday, April 12

Laura didn't come to practice today. It's the first time she's ever missed. She left a message with my mom saying she was busy. That's all. Just busy. Allie and I tried to practice without her, and it wasn't too terrible, but something was definitely missing. And it didn't help much that Allie was more hyper than usual. I realize now how Laura really helps to calm that girl down some.

"What exactly is going on with you two anyway?" asked Allie as she crammed her drumsticks back into her pack.

"I'm not sure." I unplugged my guitar and leaned it against the stand.

"I know how Laura can get on her high horse sometimes, but she usually apologizes later." Suddenly Allie grew thoughtful. "One time she told me that she does that whole judgmental thing out of habit."

"Seems like a bad habit."

"Well, you know how her church can be sometimes. I've only visited twice, but the way that preacher can go on and on kind of gives me the heebie-jeebies. It's like they're all worried about everyone blowing it, especially kids. The preacher is constantly warning everyone not to do this or that, not to make mistakes or get into trouble. It's pretty negative if you ask me."

"Yeah, I know. The only time I ever went there I felt sort of guilty for not going up to the altar when we were all supposed to 'repent.' But it just didn't feel right to me at the time. I felt like I was being manipulated. Because I honestly felt as if everything was pretty much okay between God and me that particular day. And I really didn't feel like God was asking me to go down there. The truth is, as stupid as I felt sitting in the pew all by myself and probably looking like some unrepentant sinner, I'd have felt like a hypocrite to have gone forward."

Allie pulled on her sweatshirt. "But Laura really gets drawn into all that stuff—and her parents and brother too. It's as if she's afraid to make one single mistake. Maybe it has something to do with what she told us about her older sister, the one who got messed up with crack."

"Maybe, but my brother Caleb has a drug problem too, and I don't get all freaked about—"

"But that's different."

I shrugged. "I don't see how."

"Well, you're different. And I guess you see things differently than Laura."

"Yeah, and it's okay to be different. I'm sure

not saying we all need to think alike. If Laura's happy with what she believes, I'm fine. But when she starts laying her stuff on me..." I just shook my head.

"Remember when she told us how she needs to make these big statements against sin—you know, how she went on and on about it? Well, I think it's like she's worried that if she doesn't draw these lines real dark and thick, she'll come totally unglued or something. It's like she's scared she's going to blow it really bad someday, just totally mess up her life, you know? Like if she doesn't maintain these really strict boundaries, she'll go out there and do something totally stupid and then go to hell."

I laughed. Not that it was really funny, but the way Allie said it was sort of humorous. "Yeah, I know what you mean, but I've talked to her about all this stuff before, and it seems as if she understands where I'm coming from. I've told her that I believe God wants me to reach out to every-one—no matter who they are or what they're doing. And Laura even acts as if she wants to change—wants to reach out to the down-and-outers. Then I get my hopes up, like maybe she'll step out of her little comfort zone."

"And hang with guys like Spencer and Jake and Cesar?"

"Yeah, and Marissa too." I glanced at my watch.

"Oh yeah, that reminds me—Marissa's kind of lonely, and I said maybe we could do something with her this weekend."

Allie shrugged. "Like what?"

"Good question." I looked at the rain pelting against the window. "I was thinking a bike ride, but it's pretty wet out there right now."

"Wanna go to the mall? My mom finally paid me for babysitting Davie. Man, I about fainted when she forked it over. But, hey, I didn't refuse it either."

So we called up Marissa and agreed to meet at the mall then caught the bus over there. And, looking back, despite my little spiel about Laura getting out of her comfort zone, I am so glad that she wasn't around to come with us today. If she had, I'm sure she would've said, "I told you so." And suddenly, I'm wondering if Laura might not be more right on about these things than I realized. Or not. I'm still not sure, but I'm praying that God will straighten me out on this particular one.

Okay, this is what happened. Marissa and Allie and I are walking through the mall, nothing out of the ordinary. We've already stopped by the food court to split a calorie-laden cinnamon roll; hopefully all those carbs divided by three won't hurt us too badly. And now Allie's searching for the perfect T-shirt, whatever that might be. But so far nothing's working for her.

We've just entered about the fourth store—

Madelyne's—a pretty cool clothing store with a good selection of urban styles. Allie and I usually find something pretty rad there. Anyway, we're just walking around looking at the new summer stuff and wishing the weather would cooperate a little. While Allie's rummaging through a rack of new T-shirts, Marissa and I are messing around, acting goofy and joking about an ugly new style of jeans.

Then Marissa starts playing with a basket of thongs—and I'm not talking about foot apparel. She pretends like a hot pink thong is a rubber band, like she's going to shoot me with it. Pretty funny. Then when I think she's putting it back, she scoops up a big handful of the stupid stringy things and with a completely straight face just stuffs them right into her sweatshirt pocket. Like it's no big deal.

Well, I'm speechless. I immediately glance around to see if anyone's looking or if there's a surveillance camera or anything. I'm not even sure why I do this. Although looking back now I must admit it's probably because I remember that anxious feeling—wondering if you'll get caught. And that's because I stole a pair of black leather gloves once. It was from this really nice department store that my mom likes to shop at, back when I was in middle school.

Don't ask me why I did it. It's not like I didn't

have any money. Who knows how our adolescent minds work? Oh, I probably thought I was being cool, tough, daring even. I was by myself at the time, and I never even told anyone about it—never actually thought about it much until today. But now I've decided that I'm going to put some money in an envelope (the price of the gloves) and put a note with it and just drop it off at the store.

But back to today. So, feeling a little stunned, I make this face at Marissa, a face that I'm sure says: "What the crud do you think you're doing?" But she just laughs at me, then turns and walks right out of the store. Done deal. So now I'm suddenly faced with this dilemma. What to do? Turn her in? Force her to come back? So I go over and find Allie, grabbing her by the arm.

"Come on," I urge.

"Huh?"

"Come on." I nod toward the door.

"What d'you mean?" I can tell she thinks I'm nuts. "I just found a style I like, and I want to try it on to see if it—"

"You can come back later."

"But they only have one—"

"Come on!" I take the T-shirt out of her hand, hang it back on the rack, then tug her toward the door, and we quickly exit the store.

"What on earth is wrong with you?" Allie looks seriously ticked.

"It's Marissa." I glance down the mall to spot Marissa sitting complacently next to a big palm tree planter. "She lifted some thongs," I whisper, like the FBI might be tailing us.

"Thongs?" Allie looks puzzled now. "Like rubber thongs?"

I roll my eyes. "No! Like underwear. The point is she just grabbed a handful, shoved them into her pocket, and walked out."

Well, now Allie starts laughing wildly, and frankly I don't see the humor here. "What is so funny?" I ask as we approach Marissa, who's looking pretty pleased with herself.

"You. You are acting so totally weird."

"Me? What about Marissa? What she did was wrong."

Allie nodded. "Yeah, I know that. But I swear, you're acting just like Laura right now."

Now I'm not quite sure how to react to this little comment—earlier it would have irritated me a lot—but right now I'm thinking, "Fine, at least I know Laura wouldn't shoplift anything."

"Come on, Chloe, just chill out." Allie waves at Marissa like nothing whatsoever is wrong. "Don't forget that Jesus loves everyone. Remember the thief on the cross?"

I literally stop in my tracks and stare at Allie. I am, for the second time in mere minutes, speechless—totally stopped by her words. And as

confused and conflicted as I feel inside, I suspect she is right.

But that still doesn't make this kind of thing
any easier. I know we need to forgive Marissa, but
does that make everything okay? Obviously not.
Should we have reported her? I don't think so.
Sometimes life is confusing.

HARD TO KNOW
o God
why is everything not simple?
why is life not just
plain black and white
good and bad
wrong and right?
how are we supposed to know
what to do
who to love
when to speak
when to shut up
where to go
what to think?
show me, o Lord
teach me Your ways
speak to me
in that quiet voice
that makes sense
cm

Three

Sunday, April 13

I have to admit it was kind of cool letting Allie handle the little shoplifting episode yesterday. Thinking about it now I really admire how she very calmly told Marissa that we weren't into that sort of thing.

"The truth is I've shoplifted before," Allie confessed to both of us. "At the time I kind of rationalized that it was okay because my dad had just deserted us and we were flat broke and everything seemed pretty bleak and hopeless—like who cared anyway? But then I got caught."

"You got caught?" I stared at her with fascination. "You never told me about this."

She laughed. "Hey, it's not like I'm proud of it. What really got to me was how unbelievably devastated my mom was. She was like totally crushed when they called her to come pick me up. I still remember her sitting there in the police station just sobbing like I'd murdered someone."

"What happened at the police station?" asked Marissa, apparently impressed by Allie's short-lived life of crime.

"I confessed. I mean, what was I going to do

when they'd obviously caught me red-handed? Then my mom and I had to sign some papers and agree to attend this all-day seminar about shoplifting—very boring, not to mention my mom was totally furious to miss a whole day of work. Then I had to do forty hours of community service—mostly shoveling Bark-o-Mulch at the city park. Plus I was grounded like forever, and my mom made me babysit my little brother without getting paid a penny for a long, long time."

"Whoa." Marissa looked down at her lap. "That's pretty stiff. What'd you lift anyway?"

"Just some earrings." Allie shrugged. "I think they only cost about ten bucks. But the truth is I'd stolen quite a few things before that. And I was actually starting to get pretty comfortable with the whole thing."

"Have you taken anything since then?" I asked.

"No. After going through all that crud, I didn't think it'd be worth it. Plus they promised me that my record would be expunged, that means wiped clean, if I stayed out of trouble for a year. Then, not too long after that—" she turned and smiled at Marissa—"I found God and I have a relationship with Him. And I know He wouldn't want me to steal anything."

Marissa didn't really respond to that last bit. And despite Allie's very cool lecture, Marissa apparently didn't feel the need to return her pocketful of "hot" thongs. So we pretty much parted ways, and I guess I still feel pretty lousy about the whole thing. Other than the way Allie handled it, that is. But personally, I'm still not sure what to do. I realize Marissa still needs us to love her, but I'm just not sure how I feel about hanging with her—or at least about going to the mall with her. I don't really think I'm up for that again.

But here's the good thing that happened today. I felt so bad about my fight with Laura that I wanted to talk to her <u>before</u> going to church. I remembered this time when Pastor Tony preached about how we shouldn't come to church if we were mad at someone. The Bible says that we're supposed to go take care of our problems with our brothers and sisters and <u>then</u> come to worship. So I decided to take that piece of advice seriously, and I got up early and rode my bike over to Laura's (fortunately the weather had improved).

And as I rode, I practiced what I thought I would say to her. Still, I must admit feeling rather self-conscious as I stood on her front porch so early on Sunday morning when it looked as though the rest of the civilized world was still sleeping in. But thankfully her mom was up, in a lime green bathrobe and with a cup of coffee in her hand. She acted as if she wasn't all that surprised to see me, although I suspect she was.

"You're up early today, Chloe."

"Is Laura here?"

She nodded. "I think she's still in bed, but you can go get her up if you want. You know where her room is."

So I tiptoed down the hall to Laura's room and quietly tapped on her door. I heard her sleepily say, "Come in." So I did.

Laura's head popped up from her pillow. "What are you—?"

"Sorry to wake you up." I glanced around her tidy room. Laura is a total neat freak. "Can I sit on your bed?"

She nodded with wide eyes.

"I—uh—I just wanted to talk to you," I began slowly. "I feel really bad about what happened on Friday, and I wanted to say I'm sorry. Will you forgive me?" Now I must confess that I still felt like this was as much her fault as mine, maybe even more, but then I can only be responsible for my own actions—not hers. So this is where I started. Besides, this idea had occurred to me on the way over—if you really love someone, even though you believe she's wronged you, maybe the kindest thing is for you to do everything possible to make it easier for her to say she's sorry too.

I could see that Laura was holding back tears now. She pressed her lips together as if she was thinking about what to say and then simply burst out, "I'm sorry too, Chloe. I don't know why I was being so—so—"

I hugged her. "It doesn't matter now. The important thing is we're still friends."

She nodded and wiped her eyes. "I didn't know if you'd ever want to speak to me again. I thought about calling, but I didn't even know what to say, where to begin."

"I've thought about the whole thing a lot. And maybe we should just agree to disagree about some things."

"Maybe so."

"I mean, God made us all different for a reason, didn't He?"

"I guess so."

"And just because you feel one way about something doesn't mean I have to feel the same way, right?"

"Maybe not." She still looked troubled though.

"So are we okay then?"

She sighed. "Yeah. I think so."

I glanced around her tidy room again, wondering, not for the first time, how she managed to keep everything in place. She even had an outfit all laid out for church. I'd probably just go in the jeans I was already wearing. "I guess I should probably go and let you get ready for church."

She glanced at her alarm clock. "Maybe so."

So I said good-bye to her mom, hopped on my bike, and headed home. I felt better, but I still felt like something wasn't quite right. Maybe I was still just obsessing over that stupid little episode with Marissa and worried that Laura would find out and think Allie and I were nuts for hanging with her in the first place. Or maybe I sensed something wasn't quite right with Laura. I'm still not sure. But I'm praying for Laura—that God will make her into the person He wants her to be. And me too!

MORE LIKE YOU
mold us into Your image
make us look like You
form us into Your likeness
fill our hearts anew
shape us into people
who reflect Your sweet light
grow us up and stretch us
and teach us what is right
cm

Wednesday, April 16

Today Marissa told Allie and me that she doesn't think she'll shoplift anymore. "I thought about what Allie said and figured it's probably not worth the risk of getting caught." She smiled impishly. "Still, I think I'll miss the thrill—it's such a cool rush to break the law."

Cesar was the only guy still at the table. I thought it was funny how he's always privy to these female conversations. "Sounds wise," he said. "Where I work, they really prosecute shoplifters."

Marissa laughed. "Yeah, like I'd go into Home Depot to take something. I can just see me putting a Skil saw under my T-shirt."

"Well, you'd probably get caught even if you just swiped a package of nails. They've got some pretty tight surveillance going on in there."

"Okay, I'll keep that in mind next time I want to lift a ladder or bucket of paint."

"How's your job going?" I asked, eager to change the subject.

"Pretty good. It's hard work, but I like it."

"Jake said he wants to get hired there too."

Cesar laughed. "Fat chance."

"You mean the drug test?" asked Allie.

"Yeah, among other things."

"It only takes about a week to get your system clean—that is, if you drink lots of water and take vitamins," said Marissa, as though she knew this from personal experience.

I felt my eyebrows rise ever so slightly, and I wondered if this meant she was a user too, but I didn't say a thing.

"That's not the case with weed." Cesar leaned back in his chair like he was the expert. "It'll still show up in a UA for up to a month."

"So you're staying clean then?" asked Allie.

He nodded. "Drug free and glad of it. It helps me to know they can test me anytime they like. But I don't want to go back to that. What a waste."

"Good for you." I smiled at him. Cesar really seems to have changed during the course of the school year. Okay, he might not be a Christian—not yet anyway. But he's definitely trying to live better. And he seems pretty open to a lot of the things I've told him so far. I honestly think it's just a matter of time.

"Well, maybe Jake will quit using too," suggested Allie. "If he wants to get a job, I mean."

Cesar set down his drink cup. "Yeah, my uncle says that you either quit or die. At first it sounded a little extreme to me, but the longer I stay clean—and see what my friends are doing—the more I think he might be right."

Marissa seemed quieter than usual just then, and I wondered once again if she might be into something. Although she's never admitted to anything, and she's never slipped out to smoke weed with Jake and Spencer.

"Well, the best high I've ever had is with God," I tossed in, watching for her to react. She didn't.

"Yeah, me too," said Allie. "Like sometimes

when we're jamming and stuff, singing songs for God, man, it's like way better than drugs."

Cesar leaned forward. "I remember feeling a high sort of like that once. It was really weird. I went to mass early one day, back when I was in sixth grade, and the whole church was totally empty. I just sat on this back pew and sort of listened to the silence. And suddenly I got this really cool feeling inside of me, kind of like God was right there." He laughed. "Pretty weird. But it seemed real at the time."

Marissa jumped up. "Okay, you guys are really creeping me out with all this religious mumbo jumbo. I think I've had about enough."

Allie held up her hands. "Hey, it's not as if we're trying to convert you or anything—we're just talking about stuff that's important to us."

"And don't worry," I added lightly. "We don't do an altar call or anything."

Well, Marissa kind of laughed at that, then slowly sat back down. "Okay then, I can only take so much, and just so you know, I get enough preaching from my grandparents. I mean, they're total religious fanatics who have no problem knocking me across the side of the head with their Bibles whenever they see the need. I'm sure they think I'm going straight to hell."

Just then I noticed Laura looking our way from her "safe" table with her "safe" friends, and

I felt certain that she would be somewhat shocked to hear our conversation. And that bothered me. Sometimes I feel like I'm this giant rubber band stretched between these two totally different worlds. Not that I feel guilty for hanging with the kids with problems. Fact is, we all have problems. But sometimes I feel uncomfortable being caught in the middle and I wonder why we can't all just get along—despite our differences.

DIVERSITY
You made each one
so different
so unique
our fingerprints are one of a kind
You wove our genes
so creatively
imaginatively
matchlessly
You are the Great Creator
teach me to appreciate
Your variety
Your innovation
Your diversity
And to live for Your purposes
cm

Four

Saturday, April 19

We had a great practice session today. Well, until the end, that is. Then Laura dropped her little bombshell.

"I met with my pastor last week," she told us (and I could tell by her tone that we were in for one of her minisermons). "And he thinks that our band should only do music that's glorifying to God."

I nodded. "Yeah, that's what I think too."

"Me too," agreed Allie.

Laura shook her head. "That's not exactly true."

"What do you mean?" I slumped down onto the couch, slowly closing my eyes and promising myself that I would listen to her completely—without judging or defending or getting mad. I opened my eyes in time to see Allie flop down on the couch beside me. She looked totally exasperated. But then she's been a little edgy ever since she decided to give up smoking last week—another thing that Laura could not abide. It had actually been getting pretty comical the way Allie would sneak a smoke when Laura wasn't looking, then frantically use breath spray and cologne to try to cover it up. Usually unsuccessfully.

"Okay, Laura, what gives?" asked Allie in an irritated voice.

"Well, it's hard to explain, especially to people who don't want to listen in the first place."

"Hey, that's not fair." I sat up straighter. "I want to hear what you have to say."

Laura still didn't look completely convinced. "Well, Pastor Rawlins says that everything we do should glorify God."

"Uh-huh." I nodded. "I agree with that."

"Yeah, me too." Allie leaned back and sighed as if this was a complete waste of time.

"But not all our songs are glorifying to God."

"What do you mean?" I tried to remain calm.

"What about the tree song?" she asked. "Or the Cinderella song?"

"What about them?" I tossed back.

Laura folded her arms across her chest. "They don't have one single word about God in them."

"Huh?" I blinked at her.

"God isn't _in_ them—those songs don't glorify Him at all."

I stood up. "God is _too_ in them! God is all over them, inside and out, between the lines and—well—everywhere."

"Yeah!" said Allie.

"How do you know for sure?" asked Laura.

Allie shrugged and glanced my direction. "Hey, I might not know how to explain it, but I just know it."

"Well, Pastor Rawlins doesn't think so."

"What does he know about our songs?"

"He's read all of the lyrics."

I scratched my head. Something about this felt wrong, although I couldn't put my finger on why. "Your pastor's read all my lyrics? Why'd you give him my lyrics?"

Laura looked down at her feet and twisted one of her beaded braids between her fingers (a new hairstyle that looks really cool on her). As I waited for her answer, I studied her for a long moment, and it occurred to me that she's been slowly changing her appearance—and not just for performances either. I guess I hadn't really been paying attention, but with her hair like that and wearing those low-riding jeans with frayed hems, well, she looked a lot more like us than she ever used to before. But she looks more like herself too. It's like she was trapped in this preppy look before, and I don't think it was really her.

"Yeah, why'd you give him our lyrics?" Allie stood now too. She had this defensive look on her face, and it was interesting comparing these two very different girls. Allie is so petite, blue-eyed, and blond, and sort of fragile-looking, but she was wearing her tough chick expression with her hands planted on her hips. On the other hand, Laura is taller, dark-skinned, and sturdy-looking, but the look on her face seemed to be one of intimidation.

Laura frowned. "Because he told me to."

"He told you to?" Now for some reason this just struck me as odd. Okay, I'm trying to be tolerant, to respect that different people believe differently, but this just seemed so bizarre—sort of like that George Orwell story about Big Brother. "Laura, I don't get it, why did your pastor want to see the lyrics?"

"Because he's worried about me."

Well, I felt seriously aggravated just then, but I managed to keep it under control. "Why is he worried?"

"He thinks that I'm changing, and he's worried that your doctrine might be a little—well, you know, a little off base."

"My doctrine?" I glanced at Allie for some support. "I didn't even know I had any doctrine."

Allie looked seriously puzzled now. "What's doctrine anyway?"

"It's like your religion and what you believe, I think." I looked back at Laura. "Right?"

"Yeah, something like that. Pastor Rawlins thinks yours probably isn't very biblical."

"Thanks a lot."

"It's probably not all your fault," continued Laura. "Your church's doctrine is probably off base too."

"Hey, wait a minute," said Allie. "What makes your pastor the authority on what everyone is supposed to believe anyway?"

"He's the authority for me."

I thought about that for a moment. I really didn't want to go shooting off any fireworks again. "Well, that may be true, Laura, but God happens to be the authority for me, and then, of course, there's Pastor Tony and my parents."

"That's another thing." Laura pointed her finger at me, that old scowl carved into her forehead again. "Pastor Rawlins wants to know why your lyrics always refer to God and not Jesus."

I shrugged. "I guess it's because I think of them as being pretty much the same. You know, the three in one—Father, Son, and Holy Spirit. It's easier for me to just call them God in my songs. Are you saying that's not okay with Pastor Rawlins?"

"He thinks you minimize Christ."

I blinked. "Minimize Christ?"

"I think Pastor Rawlins should mind his own business." This came from Allie, and I could tell she was about to lose it.

I tossed her a warning glance. "Maybe Pastor Rawlins should talk to me personally before he judges me."

Laura's eyes flashed. "He's not judging."

"You're telling me that he knows what I believe, but I've never had a single conversation with him. What's that?"

"It's discernment."

"So, are you saying that he discerns something is wrong with what I believe?"

She nodded, her eyes avoiding mine now.

I took in a deep breath and silently counted to ten—really I did. Getting mad would only make things worse. "My relationship with God is real, Laura, and I know I'm not perfect—"

"Who is?" asked Allie in an aggravated voice.

"I know I have lots of growing to do, and I'm learning stuff all the time. But I read my Bible every day, and I go to church, and I believe that God is teaching me stuff all the time. For sure, He uses people like Pastor Tony and Steph and Caitlin and Josh and my parents—sheesh, He even uses you guys. But the bottom line is God is the main One that I'm listening to—responding to and obeying. And if your pastor doesn't believe that, then he should come directly to me with his questions."

"Yeah, he sounds like a control freak," added Allie. "The spiritual KGB."

"That might be a bit strong," I said quickly, worried that Laura's feelings could get hurt now.

I know mine were already aching.

Laura pressed her lips together and scowled.

So I continued in what I hoped was a calmer tone. "I'm sure your pastor thinks he's watching out for your best interests, Laura. And he's entitled to his opinions. But I don't think he understands me or my music."

"Well," Laura's voice was low and husky, and her eyes were looking down again. "Pastor Rawlins told me that I can't remain in the band unless something changes."

"Like what?" I asked.

"Like you might need to start attending my church."

I just blinked at her. "You're kidding? Your pastor says I have to join your church?"

She nodded without looking at me.

"But I already have a church that I really love."

"Yeah," Allie chimed in. "Your pastor doesn't have the right to tell us what church to go to. I think there's even something in the constitution about—"

I jabbed Allie with my elbow. "Laura, do you agree with your pastor about this?"

She shrugged. "I'm not sure. But I know that I need to obey my pastor's authority."

"Well, it's your life, Laura." I looked directly at her. "But I love you and I think you're really talented, and I could be wrong, but I honestly believe God wants you to stay with Redemption, but only you can make that decision."

"But Pastor Rawlins says—"

"What is God saying to you, Laura?" My voice grew louder now. "Pastor Rawlins might be a really great guy, he might even be a great Christian—I don't know. But what I do know—and maybe this IS my doctrine—is that God is the ultimate One who can tell us what to do. Sure, he speaks through our pastors and parents and stuff, but we need to read God's Word and learn to hear God for ourselves too. Pastor Tony says we'll get messed up if we only listen to man's advice. What is God telling you, Laura?"

She didn't answer, but I could see her chin trembling and I was afraid I'd made her cry again.

"I'm not trying to be mean," I told her, feeling close to tears myself. "But I just don't understand why your pastor is coming down so hard on me. He doesn't even know me."

"I think Chloe's right," said Allie as she placed her hand on Laura's shoulder. "Pastor Rawlins can't tell us what to think or where we can or cannot go to church."

"But he's my pastor," Laura blurted out. "He wants me to be obedient to—to—"

"To God," I interjected. "God is God, and He wants us to obey Him. Pastors aren't infallible,

Laura. Pastor Tony tells us that <u>all the time</u>. He even challenges us to question him on things we don't agree with—"

"That's right," said Allie. "And he admits to the whole congregation when he makes a mistake."

"I understand how God uses pastors in our lives," I said. "Really, Laura, I go to Pastor Tony a lot for advice. And he's really good at it, but even he says that ultimately it's God who should be leading me. Don't you think that's true?"

Laura pressed her hands against her head as if it physically hurt her to consider these things. "It's so confusing."

Then I followed Allie's lead and put my hand on her other shoulder. "Laura, I think you need to talk to your parents about this too. And then go spend some time <u>alone with God</u>. Ask Him to direct you about our music and whether or not you should quit. That's all I can tell you right now. Well, that and I <u>really</u> love you."

Then Allie reached over and hugged her. And I hugged her too. We all just stood there for a long moment, huddled together in a group hug. I felt bad to feel Laura still sobbing, but maybe it's just something she needs to work through. All the while we stood there, I silently prayed. I asked God to speak to Laura, to lead her through this. And then without saying anything else, she turned away and left.

GOD ONLY KNOWS
who are we to think
we know better than God?
God blew us from dust
without Him we're nothing
useless, lifeless, emptiness
how presumptuous to imagine
we know what's best
for ourselves
for others
only God knows
He will lead
He will direct
but we need to ask
and listen
and obey
God first!!!
cm

Wednesday, April 23

Laura's been very quiet all week. Not rude or snotty. Just quiet. Like she's thinking about all this. At least I hope that's what it is. I hope she's not feeling bad because she's decided to quit the band or anything stupid like that. That would be a disaster. For one thing, the All God's Children concert is just ten days away. And if Laura quits the band, we'll probably have to cancel. But besides that, it just seems so right that the three of us are together. And if I do say so myself, Redemption really sounds great. I believe only God could do something this amazing.

Of course, I could be wrong about that. I know that just because something feels right doesn't always make it right. But we three have been through so much this past year, and everyone seems to think we have a really cool sound. It feels like things are starting to take off for us.

And I've been giving serious consideration to what Laura's pastor said about "not glorifying God with our music." I don't mean to be disrespectful to anyone, but I really don't agree. Pastor Rawlins just doesn't get it.

Still, I'm trying to put this in God's hands, because I must admit it's been making me a little nervous. I've been repeating a Bible verse to myself these past few days: "Do not be anxious about anything, but in everything, by prayer and petition, with thanksgiving, present your requests to God. And the peace of God, which transcends all understanding, will guard your hearts and your minds in Christ Jesus." The verse is found in Philippians 4:6-7, and I know it by heart.

Last night I got an e-mail from Caitlin. I'd

written to her all about this latest conflict with Laura. It was so reassuring that Caitlin felt pretty much the same as I did. Like me, she believes we need to hear and respond to God first, but she also warned me that we need good solid counsel in our lives too. That's like Caitlin, always watching out for me. And I totally agree with her about the solid counsel. I'm just not so sure that Pastor Rawlins can offer that kind of counsel for me. Besides, he's not even my pastor.

I briefly talked to Pastor Tony about this at church tonight, and he told me that he believes in a balance. "You're right, Chloe, you do need to go to God first, but you also need to read God's Word and get good advice from the leadership in your life—like your parents, pastors, teachers."

I nodded. "Yeah, I believe that too."

"But I'll admit it worries me when people try to give me too much authority over their lives."

"What do you mean?"

"Well, I've seen this happen in a couple of churches. I call it hypersubmission, but you get a very authoritative pastor and it gets to the point where the church members expect the pastor to tell them what to do about everything—I mean like where to live, who to marry, what to eat for dinner. That's not healthy."

I had to laugh. "What to eat?"

He smiled. "I know it sounds crazy. But that's

sort of how cults get started. People putting a man in the place of God." He shook his head. "I just don't ever want to go there."

"Me neither."

And I really don't. I realize I'm the kind of girl who can get overly enthused about things—mainly God-things. But I think I'd better listen to Pastor Tony and keep my life in balance. Or who knows, I might wind up in some weird cult where the pastor's telling me how to think and what to eat for dinner. Whoa, I better watch out!

WATCH OUT!
watch out, girl
don't think you're so smart
or you'll fall on your face
go flying apart
watch out, girl
ya don't know it all
you think you're so big
when you're really so small
go straight to the One
who knows what you need
listen to His voice
on His wisdom—feed
watch out, girl
keep your eyes on God
cm

Five

Friday, April 25

Okay, I just couldn't take it anymore. Laura has avoided both Allie and me all week, not to mention missing practice. So I lurked around the corner, so she wouldn't see me, then jumped out and cornered her at her locker right before lunch. "Have you made a decision?" I asked bluntly.

She kind of blinked at me. "I don't know."

I'm sure I groaned or something. "What do you mean you don't know?"

"I just don't know what to do."

"You've missed three days of practice, and we have a concert in one week! Should we cancel it?"

She sighed and looked down at the algebra book in her hand. "I don't know what to tell you, Chloe."

I swallowed and groped for words. I didn't really want to upset her, didn't want this craziness to go any further than it had. "Okay, you seem pretty confused to me, Laura," I began. She nodded. "Do you think God is confusing you?" She slowly shook her head. "Am I confusing you?"

She looked at me—steady and even, like she

was really seeing me. "No," she finally said. "I don't think you're confusing me. Actually, you've always been pretty straight with me. And part of me agrees with you."

"Is it possible that your pastor is confusing you?"

She shrugged.

"Well, I've been thinking about him—and praying. And I'm thinking since he's read my lyrics and thinks he knows what I believe, or what my doctrine is, well, maybe it's time I paid him a visit."

Now she kind of smiled in a funny little way, as if this were some kind of a joke. "Are you serious, Chloe? You'd actually go see Pastor Rawlins, like to his office?"

"Why not? I talk to Pastor Tony all the time."

She shrugged again. "Sure, go ahead, if you think it'll do any good."

So instead of going to lunch, I went straight to the phone booth and called Laura's church. First I got the secretary and I politely asked if I could speak to the pastor.

"Is he expecting your call?" she asked.

"I doubt it. We've never actually met."

"Uh-hmm." I could hear what sounded like papers shuffling.

"Look, my friend Laura Mitchell attends his church. And we have this band, and Pastor

Rawlins seems to feel there's something wrong with that. I just wanted to talk to him in person, if I could."

She cleared her throat. "Well, let me see if he has any available times."

"It's pretty urgent," I said quickly. "We have an important concert in a week, and we were donating the proceeds to charity, and I really need to—"

"Can you come by this afternoon, dear?"

"Really? Today?"

So that's how I found myself sitting in an elegant church waiting room at four o'clock this afternoon. The padded chairs were covered in dark rose-colored velvet, and the silk flower arrangements looked quite proper with every bud in perfect place. But to be honest, it reminded me a little of a funeral parlor—not that I've been to so many—but I do remember when my great-uncle Hank died, and we went to his funeral down in Shadley a few years ago. For whatever reason it felt a little like that. Only I should've guessed that today's funeral was going to be my own.

After I'd spent about twenty minutes waiting and getting seriously tired of the elevator-style religious music playing quietly in the background, the secretary told me I could go in. Now I'd seen Pastor Rawlins before, from a distance anyway, but I remembered him as a large, slightly burly white guy with a loud voice and fairly over-bearing demeanor. But the plump man shaking my hand was only a few inches taller than me, slightly balding, and he greeted me in a fairly gentle voice.

I wondered if I'd mistakenly walked into the wrong office, although I distinctly remembered seeing a brass nameplate with the correct name on the door. Perhaps the man standing before me was actually the janitor.

"You must be Chloe," he said with a soft Southern accent.

"Pastor Rawlins?"

I'm sure he saw the question in my face. He laughed. "Yes, people always think I'm bigger than I really am when I'm up there in that pulpit with my big black robes on." He pointed to a chair. "Have a seat, young lady."

I sat down and immediately noticed that my palms were sweating. Why was that? It's not as if I were guilty. Anyway, I figured I might as well jump right in and get this nasty business over with. "Laura told me that you read my song lyrics and that you're concerned that they don't—uh, glorify God."

I waited for him to say something, but when he simply nodded and said nothing I decided to just continue. "Well, I happen to think that there are all kinds of ways to glorify God. I think that my songs are about life and living and people and how ultimately we all need God in our lives. But I don't want to preach at people with my music, I just want to tell a story, to show them where I've been, where I am, and where I think I'm going." Still, he didn't say anything, and I was starting to feel flustered, like maybe this was pointless, but I kept on talking anyway.

"And now Laura is all confused and she thinks you want her to quit our band and we have a concert in a week and—" Finally I just stopped. Was this guy even listening?

He leaned forward in his chair, rubbing his palms together in a thoughtful way. "I'll admit we're a somewhat conservative church. Why, some people probably even call us fundamentalist, but we do believe the Bible to be the true and infallible Word of God, and we belong to a denomination that takes its faith quite seriously."

"I take my faith seriously too."

He smiled, but something about his smile felt insincere, although I couldn't be sure. "Now I understand you go to that new church downtown. Isn't it called a nondenominational church?"

I nodded. "Pastor Tony wants everyone to feel welcome and comfortable there, no matter what their different church backgrounds might be." I knew this for a fact since I'd recently asked him to explain what exactly that "nondenomina-tional" part meant.

Pastor Rawlins's heavy eyebrows drew together to create a deep crease in the center of his forehead, and his voice grew louder. "The role of the church is not to make everyone feel com-fortable. The role of the church is to preach God's Word, and God's Word is a two-edged sword that can cut the spirit from the soul. And believe me, child, that can get mighty uncomfortable."

I blinked and wondered how to respond to that. It's not that I disagreed with everything he was saying. I do believe the church should preach God's Word. And I don't think people should be com-fortable all the time. I know as well as anyone how it feels when God convicts you. But when Pastor Rawlins made his sword comment, I got the feeling that he'd like to slice me into tiny little pieces.

"Furthermore, God's Word is able to discern your very thoughts and the evil intents of your heart."

Well okay, I'm thinking, "Hey, get me outta here!" But at the same time I started to pray, silently begging God to help me make sense of what he was saying, what he really meant. "Look, I don't know much about that two-edged sword stuff, but I do believe that God knows everything about my thoughts and my heart and that's cool with me, but I just don't understand how you could know all these things when you hadn't even met me yet."

"God has gifted me with discernment, young lady, and I discern that you are luring Laura away from the truth with your music as well as your deceitfulness."

"Deceitfulness?" I stood up now. "What do you mean?"

"Your doctrine is deceitful, false, and full of lies. You and your church are wolves in sheep's clothing. You pretend to be godly yet you seek to devour my little lambs. I know about the festival your church put on last year, inviting all the other denominations to join in—including Jewish and Catholic."

I was speechless. I thought that Jesus' love was for everyone.

"Perhaps you noticed that our church did not participate."

Actually, I hadn't noticed since I wasn't particularly into churches at the time. In fact, I remember thinking back then, how it was odd that Caitlin's church wanted to include me, and yet that gesture alone began to break something in me.

"And the reason we didn't participate is because I discerned from the start that this was only a guise—a way to conceal your church's divisive plan to steal unsuspecting members from my congregation—"

"That's not—"

"Do not interrupt me." He stood now and suddenly seemed much bigger and taller than before. Had I been hallucinating? His voice boomed as he spoke now. "You must choose you this day whom you will serve, child, but as for me and my house, we WILL serve the Lord!"

"I serve the Lord too," I said weakly.

"You worship false gods, child."

"But I—"

"Come to my church, and you will hear God's Word preached as it was meant to be preached. Come and you will hear the truth, and that truth will set you free—free indeed."

Indeed. I just shook my head and asked myself if this guy was for real. Poor Laura. I knew I needed to say something—to respond—and I asked for God to help me. "My pastor does preach God's Word. And if you don't believe me, you should go talk to him, or better yet, come to our church and sit in on one of his sermons."

He laughed, a big booming laugh. "He's trained you well, child. Trying to recruit me—"

"I'm not trying to recruit any—"

"I see you're not ready to hear the truth. Come back to me when you're ready to be delivered from that false doctrine. All sinners are welcome at my church. But first they must confess their sins and repent of their sins. I see no repentance in you, young lady, and I must forbid Laura Mitchell from having any form of fellowship with you or your kind."

I knew there was nothing more to say, and feeling close to the brink of tears, I turned and walked out of his office. I noticed the secretary peering at me as I scurried out, and it almost seemed that she looked at me with pity. Or maybe it was my imagination.

Thankfully, the tears didn't come until I hit the street. Tears not so much for the end of our band, although that was certainly bad enough, but I felt personally assaulted and very confused. I still do. I haven't told anyone about this baffling conversation yet. I guess I'm afraid no one would believe me.

WHAT TO DO?

o God, what do i do?

confused, bewildered, hurt, betrayed

sliced and diced by the power of words

were those really Your words, God?

was that really Your truth?

no, i refuse to believe it

something is wrong

it is not of You

You have always shown me

Your love, grace, joy

peace, gentleness, compassion

forgiveness
i know who You are, God
that little man can't fool me
please, God
please, show him who You really are
and show me what to do next
amen

Six

Saturday, April 26

I called Pastor Tony this morning. I actually thought I was feeling better, but as soon as I started telling him about Pastor Rawlins, I began to cry.

"You want to come in and talk about this?" he asked in the gentlest voice imaginable.

"Do you have time?" I sort of blubbered.

"I'll make time."

So I called Allie and explained that I might be late for practice, then zipped over to the church and poured out the whole confusing story.

"I'd heard that Pastor Rawlins doesn't like us, but I thought it was probably just a rumor. A lot of that stuff goes on within the church community."

"Really?" I blew my nose on a Kleenex.

"I'm sorry to say it does. But hey, we're all human, and God is working on all of us."

"But the things he said about our church—"

"Well, that was wrong. But I think it might have to do with some of his congregation leaving his church to come here."

"Really? People have left his church?"

Pastor Tony nodded sadly. "I encouraged them to work things out and go back and talk to him. I know that some of them actually tried. And I refuse to turn anyone away. Still, I don't really enjoy being the church that people come to when they're unhappy in their home church."

"Why not?"

"A number of reasons. For one thing, I think people need to work to heal those old relationships, and maybe God can use them in their old congregation to help others to heal too, or to help the pastor to see that he's made some mistakes. Pastors make mistakes, you know. Just ask my wife." He grinned. "Also, I worry when people leave one church in anger then join another. I wonder if they might do the same thing again. I don't really want people stirring up trouble in our church either."

I nodded. "That makes sense. I do feel better now, but I don't know what to do about our band. I know Laura won't be allowed to play with us for the concert next week. Should I just cancel?"

He thought for a moment and then suddenly brightened. "I know this will sound crazy, but did you know that Willy Johnson plays a pretty mean bass?"

"I usually think of him as a drummer, since he drums for church and everything. But I can see he's pretty musical, and I suspected he plays other instruments since he's always giving us good tips."

"I know it might look a little strange, two teenage girls and an old dude, but what about asking Willy to step in for Laura, just until you get this thing worked out? I'll bet he already knows some of your songs."

"Yeah, he's helped to arrange a lot of them."

"And it's for a good cause. Chloe, I know how badly you wanted to help those Christian girls' schools in Eastern Europe."

"I really do."

And so it was Willy, Allie, and me at practice today. Okay, it felt pretty weird to start with, and I doubt we'll ever do anything more than the benefit concert, but I have to admit that Pastor Tony was right on. Willy does play a pretty mean bass.

Still, I feel unsettled about this whole thing with Laura. I mean, I didn't expect her to show up for practice, but I thought at least she would call. So I phoned her this evening and sort of glossed over my conversation with Pastor Rawlins yesterday. I guess I didn't want to make him sound too terribly bad since he is her pastor. Not that I lied, I just didn't tell her everything. But now I wonder why—why should I do anything to protect him?

"The main thing is he said he won't allow you

to play with us," I finally finished, followed by a big sigh.

"Yeah, I'm not too surprised." Her voice sounded tired and sad.

"I'm sorry, Laura. I wish it had gone differently. But the good news is we still get to do the benefit concert."

"<u>Without me</u>?" Her voice sounded more like her again. "You and Allie are going on without me?"

"It's not like we want to, Laura. More than anything, we wish you could play."

"So what are you going to do?"

"Actually, Willy is going to take your place."

"Willy?" she shrieked.

"Yeah, he's really good, Laura. He practiced with us today, and he already knows some of the songs. I'll admit he doesn't have what you have, and it'll look kind of funny, but it's for a good cause, you know."

"Yeah, I know." But I could tell she was down in the dumps again. So we hung up, and I felt bad for her, and for me, and for Redemption. I never really thought it would end like this.

GRIEVING

it feels like something died today
something I'd believed in
hoped for
dreamed of

                    prayed for
                 and now it's gone
                  sad and broken
            abandoned by the roadside
           dead and ready to be buried
                    redemption
             oh, how i will miss you
                       cm

Sunday, May 4

I haven't written in my diary for a while. I suppose I've been a little down, as well as busy practicing for the concert. We had to practice every single day just to get Willy up to speed. And yet the practicing didn't feel as fun as it used to feel. Allie felt that way too. We tried not to let on because we didn't want to make Willy feel bad, and he was being such a good sport too.

Anyway, we performed last night. Although we did okay and the crowd seemed to like us, it just wasn't the same. It was hard to get excited, and I kept feeling like a phony when I smiled because I felt like doing anything but smiling.

The good news is that we made a nice bit of money for our charity. Tony showed a few minutes of Melinda Bishop's video on the big screen. It was a street scene showing these homeless Eastern European teen girls barely making it and selling themselves as prostitutes just to buy food. Then it flashed over to the transformation after they started getting help from Melinda's Christian schooling project. The crowd really seemed to respond to these girls' needs, meaning they reached deep into their pockets. Sometimes we forget how easy we have it here in America.

But the hardest part of the evening was to spy Laura, standing all by herself over on the sidelines, just watching us perform our first couple of songs. And then she left. I didn't know if I'd be able to keep it together after that. But thanks to God somehow I did. And I must admit that Willy did his best, but something was missing. And that something was Laura Mitchell.

I don't know what we'll do now. I suppose we could look for another girl who plays bass. But what do we do? Put out a sign? Have auditions? It just seems so strange after everything seemed to fall together so easily in the beginning. Oh, I know we've had our little disputes over stupid things like songs and clothes and CD covers, but mostly we really got along well. And I think we had such a cool and unique sound. Where will we ever find that again? Still, I keep reminding myself that God can do anything. And I try not to lose hope. But tonight I'm just tired.

Oh, I forgot to mention one amazing thing that happened last night at the concert. Willy had

asked us if we wanted to give some sort of invitation after the concert, you know, give people the
chance to ask Jesus into their hearts.

"I don't know if I can do that," I told him. "I
mean, it sounds important and everything, but I'm
just not sure—"

"I'll do it," offered Allie.

I kind of blinked and looked at her funny. "Are
you serious?"

She nodded. "I think God wants me to do this."

"Well, then do it."

So right after our last song, "God's Way Not My
Way," I immediately start praying for her, and I'm
thinking I sure wouldn't want to be in her shoes
right now, but at the same time, I'm glad she's
willing. And then Allie just steps right up to the
front mike and starts talking about how she came
to know God. I mean, she goes into the whole Wicca
thing and how messed up she was and everything.
And I actually see kids down there who are crying. Kids I go to school with. So then I'm praying
even harder.

Then finally Allie gives this honest-to-
goodness altar call, only it's really sweet and
from the heart (not pushy at all), and I'm not kidding, about a hundred kids come up to the stage—
maybe more. Tony and Willy and several other
elders from our church were on hand to talk with
the kids afterward. Allie and I did too, but the

whole thing was totally amazing. Tony even had some little pamphlets ready to share that explained some basic things about the Bible. He must've known something like this was going to happen. So anyway, in spite of all this sadness about what's happened to Redemption, I'm really glad God used us last night. Even if it was our last night. And maybe that's what it was all about—just that one big night.

Thinking about that possibility makes me feel better—like it wasn't all for nothing. I need to remember that despite how things look, God is really at work. And even when it seems as though things are going sideways, if we can just trust Him, I think it'll all come out okay in the end. So that's what I'm going to believe.

PERSPECTIVES

what's upside down to me
is right side up for You
there's so much i can't see
and so much You can do
even when i'm spinning
reeling round and round
God, i know You're winning
You're my solid ground

cm

Monday, May 5

Now I may not have mentioned that most of Laura's friends go to church with her, including LaDonna and Mercedes. But none of them seem to be quite as devout as Laura. In fact, it was LaDonna who first approached me this morning.

"Your concert was so rad, Chloe!" She slapped palms with me. "Way to go, girl."

"Thanks." I glanced to see if Laura was nearby. "Actually, I'm kind of surprised you went."

She made a face. "You mean ol' Pastor Rawlins? Well, I don't let him get to me like Laura does. Man, she takes everything so seriously. Fact is, I'm thinking about leaving that church altogether. It's not as if my folks go there anyway. I can go wherever I want." She grinned. "I might even check out your church now."

Well, I forced what probably looked like a goofy smile, but I was thinking, oh, great, I wonder what Pastor Rawlins will have to say about that? "Well, you know you'd be welcome at my church, LaDonna. But I don't want it to seem as though we're trying to lure people away from their own church."

"Shoot, I've been thinking about leaving that church ever since that ol' Rawlins first started preaching there."

"How long ago was that?"

"About a year, I think." She frowned. "There used to be this real nice preacher there before Rawlins. And he never yelled and carried on like ol' Rawlins does. But I guess he was about eighty years old, and they made him retire, and we got stuck with ol' grumpy." She nodded over to Mercedes who was just coming over. "Both of us have been thinking about bailing lately."

"Hey, great concert, Chloe." Mercedes glanced down the hallway where Laura was slowly walking this way. "Better not let Laura catch me saying that." She rolled her eyes. "Or talking to you."

LaDonna shook her head. "Miss Laura isn't our boss, you know."

But Laura ignored us. Keeping her head down like she was seriously counting the tiles in the floor, she just kept going straight toward English class. But what LaDonna said about how things had changed since Rawlins came made me start thinking that maybe this heavy-handed pastor was actually holding his church hostage.

Laura pretty much avoided Allie and me for the entire day. For that matter, she seemed to avoid everyone. Or maybe they were avoiding her; I'm still not sure. But Laura looks completely miserable. And I cannot see how God would make a person live like that—so bound by fear and con-fusion and what seems to be nothing more than a modern-day slavery of the mind, not to mention the spirit. And Laura is such a good person. Really. She has the best heart, she's loving and kind, and she's a loyal friend. And yet right now, it seems as if she's in some sort of prison—like she's a victim.

But at the same time I know that Laura has a free choice in all this. I mean, it's all fine and dandy for me to think that Pastor Rawlins is the bad man holding his whole church hostage, but the fact is, they can leave if they want. He's not armed and there are no interior locks on those doors. And it's even starting to appear as if some more of his "lambs" are getting ready to bolt. I just don't understand why Laura's being so thickheaded about it. But I will be praying harder than ever. Of course, I realize it's entirely possible that I'm the one being judgmental now, because I'm sitting here thinking how Pastor Rawlins is like the devil. I mean it. I really think the man is evil. And yet he claims to be a Christian. He claims to be serving God. And so do I. And yet we are so completely and diametrically opposed. Oh, why is this so confusing?

HOW TO KNOW
who is right?
who is mad?
which is good?

which is bad?
is it feeling?
is it fact?
some hide wrong
in careful tact
use your heart
or use your mind
where to start?
what to find?
help me know
what's from above
wrapped in grace
bound with love
amen

Seven

Wednesday, May 7

I guess I haven't been as concerned with Laura the past couple days because it's like something major—I mean major—is happening at our school. A lot of the kids who were at the concert last weekend have been coming up to Allie and me and asking us questions. Some of these kids are the ones who came forward to make a commitment that night, and others are just curious about our faith in general. Anyway, it's been extremely cool.

But the coolest thing by far is what's happened with Cesar. I hadn't really noticed him at the concert that night. Probably a good thing too, since I might've been distracted by him. But Allie said she saw him there. Still, he wasn't in the bunch that came forward at her altar call. But I had noticed how he seemed more quiet than usual these past couple days, but then so much has been happening too. Then just this morning, he comes up to me in the hallway and says, "Well, I guess I went and did it."

"Huh?" I'm looking at him as if he's about to tell me he lost his virginity or something else I really don't want to hear about.

"Like Allie said last Saturday night after the concert." He was grinning now.

"You mean you made a commitment to God?" I'm sure my eyes were bugged out like a crazed frog just then. "Really, Cesar? You're not trying to put something over on me?"

He nodded. "It's for real. After work last night, I was walking across the parking lot like I always do, but for some reason—I don't even know why—I stopped and looked up at the sky. Man, you should've seen the sky last night, Chloe. It was like every star was so unbelievably bright. And I had this exact same feeling again. Remember I told you about the time in church, all by myself? It was just like that, only way more so. And I really felt as if it was God just telling me to give my life to Him. So I did. Right there in the Home Depot parking lot."

To my amazement I threw my arms around Cesar and hugged him. I'm sure I had tears in my eyes. "That is so awesome!" I stepped away feeling sort of embarrassed and silly, but I could tell he didn't mind the hug.

He smiled. "And today it's like I feel, oh, how do you describe it? Well, like I'm a whole person or something. Like before there was something missing."

"Like God."

"Yeah. Like God."

I told Allie about it, and when she saw Cesar at lunch, she nearly tackled him giving him an even bigger hug than I'd done.

"Hey, can I get some of that too?" asked Jake with a sly grin.

Allie laughed. "Aw, sure. I'm feeling so good I could probably even hug you right now." She threw her arms around Jake, and even though he'd asked for it, I could see he was a little embarrassed when all was said and done.

"So what's up with all this huggy-kissy stuff?" he asked as he sat down. "It's like we're back in the sixties and everyone's wanting to have a great big love-in or something."

"Sounds good to me," said Spencer as he sat his tray down next to Marissa. "You girls interested in a little love-in?" He nudged her with his elbow and raised his eyebrows suggestively.

"In your dreams, Spencer!"

"Hey, you can't blame a guy for trying. Besides, I feel kinda left out."

"Well, if it's any comfort, I'm not getting any either!" Marissa jammed her straw into her drink.

"Not getting any lovin'?" asked Jake in a syrupy voice. "Well, come on over here to Big Daddy, and I'll show you what I got."

"Shut up!" Marissa scowled down at her tray. "I swear you've all gone flippin' crazy. Everyone at this whacked-out school is totally bonkers these days. It's like they're all getting religion now, and it's really making me want to just puke. Seriously!" She made a face like she was about to hurl.

"Sorry," said Cesar as he sat beside her. "I guess this is partly my fault."

"Your fault?" Her voice softened slightly, and she looked at him with wide eyes. "How could it be your fault?"

"Because I've gone and done it too. Allie was hugging me just now because she's happy that I've given my life to God."

"Oh, man!" Marissa shook her head. "I don't want to hear another word about God. I just cannot take this!"

"Well, then at least hear me out," continued Cesar.

I glanced at Jake and Spencer. Would they make fun of him too? But they were both silent. Stunned, I think. Then Cesar proceeded to tell them pretty much what he'd told me in the hall. "The thing is," he finished up, "I know that this is real."

Spencer made a face. "How can you know it's real, man? I mean, it's not like you can see God or anything."

"Sometimes seeing isn't as good as feeling it inside here." Cesar tapped his chest. "And I can tell something's changed inside of me."

Jake and Spencer quickly shoved down their lunch and then dashed outside to, I'm guessing, smoke some weed and dull the truth that they'd just been exposed to. But Marissa remained at the table with us. As a result, she was forced to listen to the conversation among Cesar and Allie and me, as well as the others who dropped by to say hi or ask questions and make comments about their own personal faith journeys.

But by the time the warning bell rang, it looked as if Marissa might really be sick after all. Her face was pale and tight and I could tell she was overwhelmed and perhaps even angry. I had this feeling that if I didn't reconnect with her, she might never speak to any of us again. So I made a point to follow her to the door.

"Hey, Mariss," I said in a lowered voice. "I think I know how you feel."

She looked at me curiously. "I don't see how you possibly could."

I nodded. "Really, I think I do. I'm sure I've felt the same way. Honestly, I used to want to rip the face off of anyone who had the audacity to talk about religion to me. It would make me totally furious. Really."

"Really?"

"Yeah, you should've known me back then. I was one hard chick."

She smiled ever so slightly, then gave a tug on my studded black leather belt. "You still look pretty tough, Chloe."

"Yeah, but that's just on the outside. I'm a different person on the inside now. A whole lot happier too."

She shrugged. "Well, maybe you guys should respect that some of us heathens are just fine and dandy with the way we are. Not everyone has to get religious, you know."

"I know. And honestly, we're not going to shove anything down your throat either. You just let us be who we are, and we'll let you be who you are too. Deal?"

She seemed to think about this for a moment. "Deal."

FOR MARISSA
there's a hard shell
'round a soft heart
she's a hard sell
and a slow start
God, You can melt
though she's ice cold
the hurt she has felt
will not take hold
when Your love breaks
through her sad past
filled with mistakes

> pain that won't last
> once her heart knows
> Your love breaks through
> Your mercy flows
> and she'll love You
> cm

Friday, May 9

As soon as I found Allie this morning, I told her my plan. It may be lame, but it's better than nothing. "We cannot let this thing with Laura just keep going like this. She looks so miserable. We've got to help her."

"Yeah. I know." Allie slammed her locker shut and turned and looked at me. "So what's the answer?"

"We need to talk to her parents."

"Huh?"

"We need to ask them where they stand with this Pastor Rawlins thing. We need to find out if they know how much this is hurting Laura."

Her eyebrows shot up. "_We_? As in you and me?"

"Yeah. It's like we're representing the band, sort of."

"Hey, I might be able to stand up and talk to a crowd—I mean, like when God is leading me to—but I'm totally lousy when it comes to one-on-one confrontations involving adults, especially with parental types. You've seen me. Sometimes I even freeze up around your parents."

"My parents have that effect on people."

"Really, Chloe. I'm no good at this. I mean, I'm willing to go with you and back you up, like for moral support, but that's where I draw the line."

I patted her on the back. "Fine. That's good enough for me. I'm going to call Laura's mom and see if we can drop by this evening. I'll pick you up."

"Are you going to warn Laura?"

"I don't see what good it'll do. I think this is going to be kind of like an intervention."

"What's that?"

"You know, when someone's on drugs or something harmful to themselves, and all the loved ones come around and talk them into getting some help."

"Are you going to have anyone else come along?"

"You know that's not a bad idea. Maybe I'll ask LaDonna and Mercedes since they're actually part of the congregation."

And that is how the "intervention/insurrection" was begun.

I borrowed Mom's car then drove around picking everyone up. Allie still thinks it's unfair that I get to drive even though I'm only a freshman, but back in grade school I thought it was unfair getting held back because I was so sick that year. I guess life just balances out sometimes.

Anyway, I'd added some incentive by promising to treat everyone who was willing to come to free pizza beforehand. It wasn't a bribe exactly, just a way for us all to have a chance to sit around and discuss what we planned to do. And before we left the pizza place, we all bowed our heads and prayed for God to lead us. I knew that Laura's dad was a deacon in the church and that what we were about to do must be handled carefully—prayerfully. I also knew it could totally blow up in our faces and that Laura might never speak to any of us again—not as if that would be much different than it is now. But we were all aware of these possibilities, and we all agreed to give this thing our best shot. So at seven o'clock sharp we all stood on her porch, and I pressed the doorbell.

"Oh, my," said Mrs. Mitchell as she surveyed the crowd. "There's quite a group of you." She glanced over her shoulder then spoke quietly. "I did like you asked, Chloe. I didn't tell Laura you were coming. Is this supposed to be a surprise party or something?"

"Not exactly. It's like I said on the phone. We want to talk to you and Mr. Mitchell and Laura."

"Is it all right if James sits in? He's curious."

I heard someone giggle and remembered that

Laura had told me how LaDonna has had a huge crush on her brother for years now. "Sure, he might as well hear what we have to say too."

Soon we were all seated in the living room. And Laura looked totally stunned to see us. I know she wondered what in the world I was up to. Avoiding her eyes, I began. "We're here tonight because we're worried about Laura. But it's not just Laura. We don't understand what's going on at your church." I'm sure Mr. Mitchell's eyebrows shot up about an inch just then.

"And we don't mean to be disrespectful," I continued, "but we're really trying to figure this thing out. It's not easy to explain. You see, I went to visit Pastor Rawlins by myself, and he pretty much didn't listen to what I was trying to say—or maybe he'd already made up his mind that I was an evil influence on Laura. So I didn't get anywhere. So now we're coming to you for help. I'm sure you know that Pastor Rawlins has forbidden Laura to play in our band or even associate with Allie and me. His reason for this is because he thinks that we are corrupting her with false doctrine that's being taught in my church. But when I invited him to visit my pastor, he refused. So I don't understand how he can judge me—"

"Yeah!" interrupted LaDonna. "And I want to know just who he thinks he is to go round yelling at his congregation all the time. Just last week he told me my skirt was too short—"

"And I'm not going to church there anymore," said Mercedes. "Unless he starts being a whole lot nicer. He scares me when he shouts—"

"Hey, you guys." I waved my arms to get their attention. This was exactly what I'd asked them NOT to do. "We didn't come to—"

Mr. Mitchell loudly cleared his throat and stood. By now I halfway expected him to throw us all out of his house. "Why _did_ you come, Chloe?"

I stood and looked him in the eye, ready to speak the truth. "Because it's not right, Mr. Mitchell. God is about love and forgiveness. He's not some mean taskmaster who wants to make our lives miserable. And the songs we sing in Redemption _are_ about God and what He's done in our lives. And my church doesn't teach false doctrine. You can call my pastor and ask him for yourself—"

"Okay, okay." He held up his hands as if to stop my flow of words. "What you're telling us isn't really anything new." Then the corners of his mouth turned up ever so slightly, and I'm sure I took in a deep breath as I sat back down.

He continued. "Not that we've ever heard it put quite like that. And it might interest you to know that Mrs. Thorne, our church secretary, mentioned your little visit last week. And it had troubled her too. Well, that and a lot of other things. We've all been concerned with the direction things have been going with our new pastor, but we had wanted to give him a grace period. However, that period is over now, and the deacons and the council took a vote. It was almost unanimous—we are presently seeking to have Pastor Rawlins replaced."

Laura stood up trying to be heard amid the clapping and cheering that had erupted. "Are you serious, Dad?"

He nodded. "I guess I should've told you sooner. But it wasn't certain until just this week at the council meeting. We only informed Pastor Rawlins yesterday, and we'll have a substitute in the pulpit on Sunday."

Laura ran over and hugged her dad with tears streaming down her face.

"Well, I guess we didn't really need to come over here and make all this fuss then." I stood and sheepishly glanced toward the front door.

"No, don't feel bad." He put his arm around Laura's shoulders. "I'm glad you girls came. It's like a real confirmation. As bad as things were with Rawlins, you still feel terrible giving a man his walking papers, especially someone who's been preaching for as long as he has."

"Maybe it's time he retired," said James with a laugh.

"Hopefully, he'll let God help him through this ordeal," said Mr. Mitchell.

"You girls want something to drink?" asked Mrs. Mitchell. "I just made some iced tea."

So we all hung out for a while, drinking iced tea and chatting, and it seemed as though everything was going back to normal. But before we left I just had to ask Laura's dad something. "So, do you think it'll be okay for Laura to be back in the band again?"

He shrugged. "Well, that'd be up to her."

I turned and looked at Laura to discover she had the biggest smile I'd ever seen on her face. "You mean I haven't been permanently replaced by Willy?"

I had to laugh at that. "Willy's pretty good, but he could never replace you. I honestly don't think Redemption can continue without our original three."

"Then I'm in!" shouted Laura.

"Me too!" said Allie giving her a high five.

"Me three!" I said joining them.

And so it looks as if Redemption might not be dead after all. I'm relieved I didn't cancel any of our gigs yet. I had planned to do that this weekend, but instead it looks like we'll be practicing big-time.

And although I'm rejoicing over this, it's mixed with sorrow. The whole thing with Pastor Rawlins has been a bit sobering to me. It's not that I expect all pastors to be perfect, but I suppose I've put

them on a bit of a pedestal. Even Pastor Tony. I
need to remember that, like me, they're just
human. We all make mistakes. I suppose the dif-
ference is what we do with our mistakes. I realize
now, more than ever, that I need to humble myself
before God when I blow it. I need to accept His forgiveness and move on. I'm praying that Pastor
Rawlins does the same. I'm praying that God will
use this for Pastor Rawlins, and maybe he'll be a
whole lot happier in the end. He sure didn't seem
very happy to me the other day.

BLESSED REDEEMER
thank You, God
praise Your holy name
You are so amazingly
incredibly, powerfully, almighty
God
thank You
for redeeming
redemption
and me
amen

Eight

Thursday, May 15

Marissa seems to have really warmed up this past week. It's as if she suddenly has this keen interest in listening to our conversations—no more of the "you're making me sick" talk. So I'm feeling hopeful that God is really doing something in her after all. Not only that, but Laura's gotten a lot more open to hanging with a wider variety of people. It's as if she's not scared anymore.

Oh, I know that Jake, with his weird tattoos and lip rings, and Spencer, with his obvious drug habits, make her a little uncomfortable sometimes, but Laura's actually managed to eat lunch with us twice this week—and been friendly. And she seems fairly impressed with what's going on with Cesar. What's even more surprising is how she and Marissa have made some sort of connection. Talk about your opposites. So anyway, when Marissa asked if we three wanted to go hang at the mall with her after school, before Allie and I could speak up, Laura said, "Sure, sounds fun."

Naturally, I was thinking, "Uh-oh, this could be trouble. Should I warn Laura about our last adventure in the mall with Marissa? Then again,

Marissa had sworn off shoplifting." Anyway, when I met Laura after school, she was so excited—and in a very un-Laura-like way acting like a total chatterbox—that I never got the chance to warn her. Besides, I was curious as to what was up.

"Guess what?" she said as we walked toward her bright yellow Neon to meet Allie and Marissa.

Well, I hate those 'guess what?' games. "Let's see...you've decided to dye your hair pink?"

She laughed. "Oh yeah! No, I was coming out of my algebra class, and Ryan Hall said hi."

Now I had to laugh. "<u>That's</u> your big news, Laura? That Ryan said hi?"

Of course, I should know better than this because Laura's told me, in sworn secrecy, that she's had a crush on him since grade school. Ryan Hall is a good friend of her brother James, not to mention a great athlete who probably has several college scholarships being tossed his way. Even a freshman like me knows all this. But anyway, I decided to play along with her. "So, did you say hi back to him?"

"Of course, silly. And then he kept talking. He told me that he'd heard some good stuff about our band."

I smiled now. "Really? What does he think?"

"He thinks it sounds pretty cool. But he really

wants to hear us play. So I invited him to the Paradiso on Saturday." Just then Allie and Marissa walked up, and we all piled into Laura's car, and although I exchanged glances with Allie, it was too late to say anything else.

But when we got to the mall, I locked eyes with Al and said that I was going to the rest room. Fortunately, she got my telepathy and trailed after me while Laura and Marissa waited for us.

"Should we say anything to Marissa?" asked Allie.

"I don't know. I wanted to tell Laura about Marissa's little habit, but I didn't get the chance."

"Me neither."

"But Marissa did say she's not going to do it anymore, remember?"

"You think she really meant it?" Allie glanced to the door as an older woman came in.

I shrugged. "I don't know."

"Maybe we should just trust her." Allie was whispering now, and the older woman kept eyeing us both suspiciously as she pretended to rummage through her purse. I wondered if she might actually be an undercover security guard—and suddenly I started feeling guilty, which was totally weird. I shook my head and told myself that I was getting ridiculously paranoid.

"Yeah," I said. "We're probably worried about

nothing. Let's get out of here."

So we went out, and the four of us headed over to the food court to get a snack. Then we started walking through the mall, hitting our favorite shops and just talking and joking around like normal. And as far as I could see, everything was perfectly fine—no sticky-fingers, nothing coming down. We were just getting ready to leave when I sighed in relief. Marissa had minded her manners. Of course, I didn't see everything. Who ever does?

We had just left Hodge-Podge, an accessories store that's really sort of lame and preppy, and were about to exit from the mall when a man in a jean jacket stopped us. I thought maybe he was asking for directions at first, and then I got scared.

"Come with me," he said with a stern voice. Now I honestly thought this dude was trying to kidnap us. Pretty bold move to get four girls at once.

"No way!" I said, stepping up to him like the tough chick that I can be if I need to.

Then he opened his jacket, and I thought he was going to pull out a gun. I think my knees got a little weak just then. But instead he pulled out a badge. "I'm with security, and we think you girls have been shoplifting."

I glanced at Allie and she looked at Marissa.

"We most certainly have not!" Laura stepped up

beside me now, and I could tell she was really irritated.

"Look, girls, you can come willingly and make this a whole lot easier or..." He now had a little radio that he was talking into, something about possibly needing police backup.

Laura's eyes narrowed. "Fine. But I expect a full apology when you find out you're wrong."

I couldn't take my eyes off of Marissa. But her face was completely void of emotion. Whether she was scared, angry, guilty, or whatever, there was no way to know for sure. We were then taken back to Hodge-Podge and through the store, where a couple of onlookers paused to stare, like we were some kind of criminals, a gang or something. He led us into the back room, where the overly made-up clerk was waiting with a stern look on her face. "Yep," she said smugly. "That's them."

"What are you talking about?" demanded Laura, her dark eyes flashing like burning coals. I don't think I've ever seen her that angry before.

The clerk turned to the undercover security dude. "Can you handle this? I need to go watch the till right now, but I'll call the cops from out there."

"This is totally absurd," said Laura. "I demand to—"

"Look, ladies, if you don't have anything to

hide, then you probably won't mind if I check your backpacks and purses. If you're innocent, you can be on your way with my apologies."

"Fine!" Laura slammed her purse onto the table in front of us. "But I think this is a case of plain harassment, and you guys could be in big trouble. My uncle is an ACLU attorney."

Allie and I exchanged glances as we slowly set our packs on the table. The officer was going through Laura's oversize purse now, but Marissa still had her bag slung over her shoulder, her arms folded across her chest as she just blankly watched everyone. It's almost as if she were simply a spectator there.

"What's this?" The security officer pulled a lime green scarf from Laura's purse as if he'd just done a magic trick. The sales tag was still dangling from it. I could read the price of twenty-four dollars from where I stood.

I've never seen Laura's eyes so big. "What? Wha—" she sputtered then recovered. "That is NOT mine."

He nodded grimly. "Yes, that's the whole point."

"Bu-but, I didn't—"

He interrupted her by reading the Miranda rights from a note card he just pulled from his pocket. Then he turned to our backpacks. "Mind if I have a little look-see here too?"

I shrugged and the next thing I knew he was

pulling his little magic trick again. Only this time it was a hot pink scarf coming from my pack. And the next one was a purple one from Allie's. The three scarves were splayed across the table like some sort of hideous rainbow. I turned and glared at Marissa.

"Next?" the officer held out his hand for her purse.

Without saying a word, she handed it over, but after a quick search he found nothing. He handed it back. "Pockets?" he asked. Then she pulled out her jean pockets and showed him her jacket pockets until finally he seemed satisfied. "Okay, I guess you're free to go."

"Wait just a minute," I said quickly. "Marissa, what IS going on here?"

She just shrugged. "See ya later."

"Marissa!" demanded Allie. "You are going nowhere."

"Quiet!" said the officer. "You three sit down and shut up. The police will be here in a few minutes."

"This isn't fair—"

The guard stuck his finger in my face. "I said quiet!"

So as Marissa ducked out the door, we three sat in stunned silence as the guard removed our various ID cards from our bags and wallets and began writing down names and addresses as if we weren't even there. What did he think? That if he asked us we would give him false ones?

Marissa had obviously planted those stupid scarves in our bags, but why? Did she really hate us that much? Just when I thought we were getting somewhere with her too. You never know about people. But to think that she was off the hook—outta here just like that—totally infuriated me. I had absolutely no doubt that she had framed us! And I was so enraged that my fingernails were digging into my palms, but I knew I'd better do as the security officer had said. Keep quiet. Otherwise I'd say something totally regrettable.

Then I heard this little snuffling noise to my left and turned to see Laura sitting there quietly crying, tears running down both cheeks, and suddenly I felt totally guilty. As if this were somehow my fault. After all, I'd been the one to originally befriend Marissa, and then I'd encouraged Laura to reach out to kids who were searching. And now look where it had gotten us today! I felt like total crud. Perhaps Pastor Rawlins had been right about me all along.

And yet I was still furious at Marissa too. Holding back my own angry tears, I put my arm around Laura and whispered, "Don't worry, it'll be okay." And then I turned to see Allie on my right. Her face looked pale as a sheet, as if she were in

shock, but her head was bowed down, and I could
see her lips moving. I knew she was praying.
Suddenly I remembered about getting her record
expunged and how this would ruin everything.
Still fuming, I decided I better follow her lead.

It seemed like an hour before the police
arrived, although I suspect it was only a few minutes. It was a woman officer, and for some reason
this made me feel just a tiny bit better. She went
out of earshot to talk to the security officer
then came back to us. "So is this some kind of a
game?" she asked us.

"Huh?" this from Allie.

She picked up the three gaudy scarves. "This. I
seriously doubt that you girls actually wanted
these—uh—colorful scarves. Tell me the truth, are
you girls in some new sort of club or gang? Was this
some sort of an initiation or a dare or something?"

I stood up now. "You want to know the truth?"

"You've had your rights read to you?"

I nodded. "The other girl—the one who was
released, well, I don't mean to be a snitch or anything, but we happen to know she shoplifts—"

"What?!?" said Laura.

"Yeah, I'm so sorry, Laura." I turned back to the
policewoman. "Anyway, Allie and I were with her
once before when she stole thongs, and we tried to
get her to take them back, but she wouldn't. Then
we talked to her about it at school, and finally she

told us she wasn't going to do it again."

The officer was writing something down.

Allie stood up now. "It's true. It was about a month ago. She went into Madelyne's and stole a whole handful of thongs—"

"You mean like flip-flops?" the officer looked at Allie skeptically.

"No, I mean like underwear." Allie shook her head hopelessly. "Oh, I'm sure you don't believe us."

"Excuse me," the store clerk stuck her head in the doorway and motioned to the policewoman. "I need to talk to you."

"You girls stay put," said the officer, heading out the door.

"You knew Marissa shoplifts?" said Laura in a horrified tone. "And you came to the mall with her again?"

"It's like I said..." I couldn't make myself look at Laura. "She'd told us she wasn't going to do it anymore."

"And don't forget, Jesus forgave the thief on the cross." Allie spoke in a weak voice, as if even she didn't quite believe it anymore.

Laura just slumped over in her chair, placing her head in her hands. "God help us."

Suddenly Allie started to giggle, and the next thing I knew she was humming one of our songs— the one called "God help us." So, feeling generally lame about everything, I started singing along quietly with her, and before long Laura joined in too. And, well, it was actually pretty cool—the three of us sitting there in our little backroom dungeon, just singing away in three-part harmony. And before long, as strange and goofy as it sounds, we were actually smiling too.

That's when the policewoman and security guard walked back in. "What's going on here?" asked the guard. "You girls turn the radio on?"

I smiled. "Sorry, we were just singing."

He frowned. "That sounded pretty good."

"That's because we're in a band."

"A band?" the policewoman asked.

"Yeah, we're called Redemption. It's a Christian band actually," offered Laura, shaking her head. "Which must sound a little weird in light of all this."

I had to giggle now. "Look, as God is our witness, we did NOT take those scarves. Honestly, we didn't. But we totally understand how we must look pretty guilty—getting caught with them right in our bags. Maybe you should just let us call our parents." Yet even as I said this the prospect of explaining this whole thing to my parents sounded grim. And poor Allie. She'd been through this already. Laura looked horrified, and to be honest, I suppose I was more worried about how her parents would react to me than my own. I'd barely won their respect. And now this.

"Well," the policewoman began slowly. "It seems the clerk is backing your story now. She said it was the girl with the long dark hair that she'd actually witnessed lifting the scarves, but she just figured you were all involved. But the security camera will tell us the whole story." She looked at me now. "What's this girl's name?"

I swallowed hard. I've never liked being a snitch, but at the same time, I knew we must cooperate. "Marissa."

"Marissa what?"

I scratched my head and turned to Allie. "You know, I don't even know her last name. She just moved here about month or so ago. Allie, do you know?"

Allie shook her head. "Just Marissa."

"Do you know where she lives?"

"I don't. Do you, Al?"

She shook her head again. "I guess we don't really know too much about her."

The policewoman frowned. "Maybe you should be a little more careful in how you choose your friends."

Laura chuckled now. "Yeah, that's what I'd been trying to tell them."

"But Jesus wants us to love everyone," said Allie.

"Well, that's nice," said the policewoman. "But I'm sure Jesus doesn't want you to get into trouble doing it."

"Are we in trouble?" I asked.

She closed her book. "Not today. But let this be a lesson to you."

"You mean we can go?" asked Laura.

The policewoman nodded. "We'll check out the videotape to make sure it matches your stories. Then we'll try to track down this mysterious Marissa chick, but for now you're off the hook."

Allie sighed loudly. "Thank God!"

Once again, I realized that she probably had the most at risk here, since she'd been caught stealing before. And for her sake I was hugely relieved.

"Hey, are you the kids who did that concert at the festival a while back?"

"Yeah, mostly," I said. "Laura missed out on it."

"But I'll be at the next one," she said.

"When's that?" asked the policewoman.

I grinned. "Well, these two haven't exactly heard about this yet. But the pastor at our church wants to have sort of a memorial concert for his brother and the other kids who were shot at McFadden two years ago. He asked us to play. If all goes well, it'll be at the park on Memorial Day."

"I'll try to make it," she said. "In the meantime, you girls stay out of trouble. Okay?"

We promised we would do our best and then thanked her and got out of there as quickly as we could without drawing any further attention to ourselves. And I cannot even begin to explain how good it felt to get out of that stuffy old mall and breathe the clean, fresh air again.

I'm not sure what we'll do about Marissa. Right now I'm trying not to be too furious at her. After all, we _are_ supposed to love our enemies— and forgive. And God did step in and rescue us at the last minute. Whew!

FREE INDEED!
Like those three in the fiery furnace
we awaited our fate
unjustly charged
framed and persecuted
and then You joined us there
and You comforted us
You brought us joy
and hope and light
and finally we were set free
but freedom only comes through You
Your life, Your truth, Your spirit
are what set us free
and we are free indeed!
Thank You for showing up
again and again and again
amen

Nine

Monday, May 19

Marissa hasn't been at school for two days now. I wonder if she fled the country or is just waiting for us to cool off. Or maybe she's just lying low because she thinks the police are on the lookout for her.

"You think she's afraid to face us?" asked Allie as we sat down to lunch at our old table.

"Yeah, she probably thinks we're going to beat her to death with our Bibles." I took a sip of soda.

"Who're you talking about?" asked Jake.

"Aw, nothing." The three of us had agreed not to talk about this to anyone.

"Are you talking about Marissa?" asked Spencer suspiciously.

I just stuck my fork into my salad.

"I saw her yesterday," said Spencer, using this piece of information like a baited hook and waiting for us to bite.

I glanced at him, trying to decide if he was telling the truth or not. "How's she doing?" I asked nonchalantly.

He shrugged. "I dunno. She seemed a little nervous to me."

"How's that?" I focused my attention on stabbing a cherry tomato before it leaped from my plate.

"I think she's freaked about something."

I looked up at Spencer. "What did she say exactly?"

"She asked if the cops have been at school looking for her."

"What'd you say?" asked Allie.

He shrugged again. "Haven't seen any cops around."

"So?" This came from me.

"Then she asked if you guys had said anything about her."

"And?"

"I said not that I recalled." He narrowed his eyes. "Just what's up with you guys anyway?"

I tried to act dumb. "I dunno."

"Come on, Chloe, what gives? Are you guys in some kind of trouble?"

Now, here's what's ironic, and maybe this is one way to tell a real friend from one who isn't. But when Spencer asked if we were in trouble, it's like his eyes lit up, and I could tell he was really hoping we were. Like that would be a really good thing. And that bugged me. "Did Marissa say we were in trouble?" I asked.

"Not exactly. But I'm thinking you are." He turned to Allie. "Come on, Al, you can tell me.

What'd you good little Christian girls do to get in trouble with the law?"

Just then Cesar joined us. He looked puzzled. "You guys are in trouble with the law now?"

I had to laugh. "See!" I pointed my fork in the air. "This is just how rumors get started."

"What's he talking about then?" asked Cesar.

"Beats me," I said. "Ask Spence."

Spencer rolled his eyes. "I give up." He nudged Jake. "You wanna go get some fresh air?"

But Jake shook his head. "Nah."

Spencer looked crushed. "Whad'ya mean?"

"I just don't wanna is all."

Spencer slammed his drink cup down and stood. "Fine! You sit here with the goody-goody kids." Then he cussed and left.

Jake was still looking down at his tray, not even touching his cheeseburger, which he usually devours in about four bites.

"You okay, Jake?" I asked.

"Yeah."

"You don't sound okay," said Allie.

"What's up, man?" asked Cesar.

Jake looked up at us and sighed. "You guys wouldn't understand."

"Hey, why don't you give us a shot," I said. "Between the three of us, we've been through a lot more than you think."

He shook his head and tugged at one of his lip

rings. "You haven't been through this."

"Does it have to do with your stepmom?" asked Allie.

The way his eyes flashed, we knew she'd hit the bull's-eye. But still he didn't answer.

"Is she coming on to you again?" asked Cesar in a very calm and matter-of-fact voice.

We were all silent now. Poor Jake. I could tell he was embarrassed. But I must admit I felt kind of astonished. I mean, I'd heard him rag about his stepmom before, but I never suspected anything like this. And for the first time since I'd met him last fall, I felt really sorry for him. But who would've guessed that this tough-looking guy with lip rings that resemble fangs and his weird dragon tattoo—could be hurting like this?

"She's such a tramp," he finally said. "I still can't believe my dad married her right after Mom died."

"Your mom died?" I asked.

He shrugged. "Yeah, it's been a couple years now."

"Well, can't you just tell your stepmom to bug off?" asked Allie indignantly.

He laughed. "Sure, but then she makes my life hell."

Cesar turned to him. "So, are you actually—?"

"Butt out!" snapped Jake, but his face turned

as red as his hair. Then leaving his food untouched, he took off.

"Man, I shouldn't have said that," said Cesar.

"You didn't do anything—"

"No, it was wrong to talk about that in front of you girls. I'll go find him." He stood up, pausing to pick up both his and Jake's untouched burgers. "You better be praying for us."

Allie and I both nodded, still somewhat stunned, and then we watched Cesar streak across the cafeteria behind Jake.

"Sheesh." Allie shook her head. "Guess we know how to clear a table."

But then we did something we've never done before. Right there in the midst of the noisy cafeteria, with music blaring so loudly we could barely hear ourselves, we bowed our heads and prayed for Jake and Cesar. It's not like we said so much, but it felt very real. And it was the weirdest yet coolest thing. Really!

Even now, I can't exactly remember what we prayed. But then we finished and we said amen and then looked around to see if everyone was staring at us. Not that we cared too much. But no crowd had gathered to watch the amazing spectacle—headline reads: Two Girls Pray in High School Cafeteria—and so we just quietly ate our lunch.

POUR IT DOWN
pour it down, God
pour down Your love
pour it down, God
mercy from above
pour it down, God
for everyone to see
pour it down, God
pour it down through me
amen

Tuesday, May 20

After we finished practice this afternoon, we told Laura, without giving any details, that everyone needs to be praying especially hard for Jake right now. He didn't show his face in the cafeteria today, even though Cesar said they'd had a pretty good talk yesterday.

"And pray for Cesar too," I reminded them. "Since he's trying to help him."

"That's so amazing," said Laura. "In the first place, I never imagined someone like Cesar would get saved, but Jake—now he seems about the least likely of anyone."

"Goes to show you never know."

"Sounds like a song starting up there," said Allie.

I smiled. "Maybe so."

"Hey, have you guys seen Marissa around?" Laura asked suddenly.

We both shook our heads.

"I've been thinking about her," Laura continued. "And praying for her too."

"Well, I'm trying to forgive her, but I'm still pretty mad at her," confessed Allie. "I'm kind of relieved that she hasn't been at school. I'm afraid I'd give her a big ol' chunk of my mind."

"I just hope she's okay," said Laura. "I really want to tell her that I forgive her."

"Really?" I studied Laura curiously. For some reason, probably old stuff from the past, I figured Laura would be the last one to forgive Marissa.

"Yeah. She needs to know we've forgiven her."

"You're right," I said. "I guess we should all tell her that—if we ever see her again, that is."

Allie rolled her eyes at me. "Yeah, yeah, I know you guys are totally right on, and I know that's what we're supposed to do. And I will, eventually. But, sheesh, I don't get why she had to do that in the first place. What'd we ever do to her? It was just so incredibly mean, not to mention totally lame. And man, I still think about how I could've gotten into so much trouble if it hadn't gotten cleared up."

"That's right." Laura shook her finger at Allie. "I forgot that you're a repeat offender."

"An innocent repeat offender."

"Well anyway," continued Laura, "I've been praying real hard that God will really use this in her life, and I believe that He will."

"That's cool. I guess we should all pray for that."

Then we talked some more about what was going on in school, and Laura came up with the idea of starting a Bible study. "You know, so many kids have been asking me about stuff, and some of them don't know anything about the Bible."

"Isn't it illegal to do that at school?" asked Allie.

I laughed. "That's so hilarious, if you think about it. I mean, considering the other stuff they teach us like sex ed and philosophy and evolution. And then they won't let us have a Bible study?"

"I'm not sure that we can't have a Bible study at school," said Laura. "I'll check it out with the counselor. But if we can't have it on campus, maybe we could have it at my house. That's pretty close to school."

"Would your parents mind?" asked Allie.

"I'd think they'd be glad."

"By the way, how's it going at your church these days?" I asked.

"It's been totally cool. Everyone's so relaxed and happy again. Just like it used to be."

"You think some of your old congregation will come back?"

"I hope so. I heard some of them had been

going to your church during the past year."

"Yeah, but if things have changed, I'm sure Pastor Tony will encourage them to go back."

She smiled brightly. "Well, tell him things have changed!"

"I'll say," agreed Allie. "But I think you've changed too, Laura. I mean, you're so totally happy. You're like Suzy Sunshine again."

Laura beamed. "Well, I was wondering how to tell you guys this..."

"What?" I demanded.

"Ryan asked me to the prom!"

"You're kidding?" Allie's eyes got big. "You're going to the prom! I am so totally jealous!"

"When did this happen?" I asked.

"Remember when I stayed later at the Paradiso after we finished up on Saturday night? I stayed to talk with James and Shauna, and, well, Ryan was sitting with them. And Shauna went on and on about how much fun the prom would be, and then James gave Ryan a bad time for not having a date. Then totally out of the blue he asked me!"

"That is so cool!" I shook my head in amazement. "Do you have a dress yet?"

"Mom and I are going shopping tonight."

"Talk about cutting it close," said Allie. "Isn't the prom on Friday?"

"Yeah, but I felt kind of funny telling you guys since I knew you weren't going."

"How do you know I'm not going," said Allie in her sarcastic voice. "I'm certain that Taylor Russell is about to ask me any day now—in fact, I better hurry home now just in case he called."

I had to laugh since Taylor's about the most popular guy in the junior class. Even if I do think he's a complete jerk. "Yeah, sure, Allie. Just get in line with the other starry-eyed chicks like Tiffany Knight."

"Yeah, Tiffany wishes!" Allie glared at me.

"Oh, Allie might have a chance with Taylor." Laura had a twinkle in her eye. "I mean, everyone knows he takes out a new girl every week. Maybe this is Allie's week."

"Well, I can see why he has his choice of girls," Allie made a goofy face. "Like he is such a hottee!"

I rolled my eyes. "Hey, Al, I thought you had a crush on my brother, you used to think that he was such a hottee."

"Yeah, but Josh is taken."

"Not right now," I reminded her. "Remember I told you how they broke up."

She laughed. "Well, he's really a little old for me, doncha think?"

"Yeah. Better stick with Taylor," said Laura. "Besides, he's probably sitting in front of your door right now just waiting for you to get home."

So I'm sitting on my bed wondering if Laura is

going to get all serious with Ryan now. Not that he's a bad guy. He actually seems really nice, and he goes to their church and has known their family for years. But I've always appreciated that Laura's such a sensible girl, and now she seems all romance-struck and gah-gah. I just hope she's not in love.

I know it shouldn't bug me like this, and I'm certainly not jealous. Okay maybe just a little jealous because sometimes I think it sounds pretty cool to have a boyfriend—I mean a <u>good</u> boyfriend, not a jerk. But the main thing that's worrying me is that I don't want Laura's new "love interest" to mess up things for Redemption. Especially when it feels as though we're about to take off. I know it's totally selfish. It's not as if music is my complete life, and I don't want to be consumed by it. But it's pretty important.

YOUR WILL ALONE
Your will
not mine
Your will
divine
Your will
obey
Your will
today
amen

Ten

Friday, May 23

It's prom night. Big deal. Okay, I know it's supposed to be important, but I'd just like to know why? Why do people want to spend lots of money to dress up in stupid outfits that they'll be embarrassed to admit they ever wore in few years? Or go to some overpriced restaurant where they pretend to have manners (or not), then briefly dance to a second-rate band before they start slipping out to get drunk or high or mess around and hopefully not end up pregnant?

All right, I know I must sound like Miss Sour Grapes, but really I couldn't care less about the prom. But to Laura, and half the kids at school, it's like they're planning some big trip to Paris or their weddings. I just wish everyone would come back to earth. Maybe it'll all blow over by next week, when it's nothing more than a memory. Although I'm sure Allie and I will have to hear all the details of Laura's big night with Ryan first.

Allie is spending the night tonight. She's actually a little bummed that she didn't get invited to the prom. Give me a break. But I'm pretending to care, well, sort of. Mostly I'm trying to distract her from feeling too sorry for herself and thinking she needs to find a boyfriend. Anyway, it's really late and she actually fell asleep, which is pretty weird since she's normally the hyped-up one and I'm usually the one who drops first. But then, she said she had to get up early this morning to help with Davie when he woke up with a nightmare. So I guess the poor girl's zonked.

As I'm sitting here thinking how stupid the prom is, I am suddenly so thankful that school's going to be out in only two weeks. I'm sick of it. Really. Oh, I know some great things are happening—and that's cool. Lots of kids have come to God in the past several weeks, and the climate there is definitely improving. But I'm just tired of the same old grind. I'm ready for a break, and I am really looking forward to having more free time to work on music.

I just hope Laura and Allie will cooperate. Laura's talking about working more hours at the vet clinic, and tonight Allie said she's going to get a job somewhere—anywhere—even at McDonald's if she has to. McDonald's? I think she's losing it. But she says if she gets a "real" job her mom can't force her to babysit Davie all summer.

Hey, I'd much rather babysit Davie than sling greasy hamburgers all day long. And I realize it's not because he has Down's syndrome that she's saying this. I know how she just doesn't like being stuck in the apartment so much. And after all, it's her life. I just wish there was a way we could somehow make enough money playing music so that neither of them would have to work at all. We could just spend our time practicing. So cool.

But the reason I'm writing at one in the morning is to report on what's happened this week. It's actually been quite interesting. I'll start with Marissa, that amazing and disappearing kleptomaniac.

On Thursday, after we've almost decided that she's moved to another planet, Allie and I spot her, and she's sitting at our old table. We were about to join Laura and her friends but decide we better not miss this opportunity.

"Marissa's over there," I whisper in Laura's ear.

Her eyebrows shoot up, and the next thing I know she picks up her tray. "Let's join her."

So the three of us head over to where Marissa is sitting with Jake and Cesar. Spencer's been kind of out of it lately—keeping his distance. I think he blames us that Jake is suddenly not so interested in smoking dope with him. But then Jake is really trying to sort out his life right now, and Cesar has really stuck by him this week. Cesar is such a cool guy and a loyal friend too.

He's even letting Jake stay at his house for a
while until Jake figures stuff out. It's hearing
this kind of crud about families (like Jake's) that
suddenly makes me appreciate my parents a whole
lot more. Oh, sure they have their problems and
they're a little checked-out and slightly self-
absorbed sometimes, but compared to some they're
pretty great. Okay, back to Marissa.

"Hi, Marissa," says Laura, as if everything's
peachy. "Where you been?"

"Around." Marissa intently studies her french
fries as she squeezes ketchup all over them like
she's creating modern art.

We sit down and I can tell the guys are waiting
for something exciting to happen. Without knowing all the details, they both know something's
up between her and us.

"So, been to the mall lately?" asks Allie in a
light tone.

Without looking up, Marissa just shrugs and
selects a long fry.

Now, I'm trying to think of something to say
that will cut through this ridiculous game playing but am basically coming up empty.

"Marissa..." Laura begins in a gentle voice.
"We're—uh—wondering about something." She
pauses to glance at the guys. "But maybe you'd
rather talk about this privately."

Marissa just shrugs again. "I don't care."

"Okay, then," Laura continues more firmly. "We're pretty confused about what you did to us at the mall last week."

Allie rolls her eyes. "That's putting it mildly."

Marissa then looks up at Allie. "Hey, I didn't mean for that to happen."

Allie laughs, but it's her hooting laugh, the one that's saturated in sarcasm. "Oh, yeah! I suppose you accidentally stuffed all those stupid scarves into our bags, right?"

Marissa looks from Allie to Laura. "It was supposed to be a joke."

"A joke?" Allie slaps the table. "And a pretty funny one too."

"Allie." Laura tosses her a look. "Marissa, do you have any idea what kind of trouble you—"

"Look, I'm sorry, okay? It was really stupid. Honestly, I didn't think we'd get caught. I was going to wait until we were all outside, out in the parking lot, and then I was going to—"

"But you just took off!" I'm no longer able to contain myself. "You didn't even stick around to explain what the—"

"I know. I know." Marissa looks up now with what appear to be real tears in her eyes. "It was wrong, okay? I didn't mean for it to go like that. I was trying to be funny. But you guys just don't understand."

"We don't understand?" Allie sounds seriously fried now. "Marissa, I'd already told you I have a history—like what did you think—?"

"I'm sorry! I'm sorry! Okay? Crud, what more can I say?" She pushes her tray away, puts her head down on the table, and really starts crying.

Okay, now I'm starting to feel pretty bad. I mean, here we'd talked about all this forgiveness, the thief on the cross, and we've suddenly turned into the Spanish Inquisition.

Fortunately, this is when Laura reaches over and puts a hand on Marissa's arm. "Well, God was watching out for us because we didn't get into trouble."

Marissa looks up. She has two dark streaks of mascara and eyeliner running down her face. "You didn't?"

"The clerk finally told the police that you were the one she'd seen, and it was all on the video cam as proof."

I glance over to see how Jake and Cesar are taking all this. Do they think we're nuts? But they're both just quietly eating their lunch and listening, it seems, with real interest.

At first Marissa looks somewhat relieved at Laura's news, but then she gets this slightly horrified expression. "You mean I'm on the video cam?"

"That's right," says Al, and I think she's

enjoying this moment a little too much. "So they let us go."

"I'm glad they let you go." Marissa sniffs, then wipes her nose on a stiff paper napkin.

"They asked us your name," continues Laura in an even voice.

"Did you tell them?"

"Just your first name," I offer. "None of us even know your last name."

Marissa sighs. "It's Malone. You might as well know. Marissa Anne Malone."

"So we can turn you in?" asks Allie, but there's no more smugness in her voice.

"Whatever." Marissa wads the napkin into a tight little ball. "I don't really care anyway."

"You _want_ to get caught?" Now Allie leans forward with fresh interest. "What? Are you nuts?"

Marissa shrugs. "Yeah, maybe." Then she looks evenly at us. "You may as well know—my dad's a cop. And if I get caught, he'll throw a total fit."

"Your dad's a cop?" Allie's eyes are practically bugging out of her head now. "And you _want_ to get caught? Man, you _are_ crazy!"

Now Marissa gets this tough look on her face—it's an expression I can personally relate to because I've worn it so many times myself. "Look, you guys," she says. "I'm really sorry about that whole scene. It was totally, totally moronic. I wish I'd never done it, okay? But that's who I am, understand? I do stupid stuff without thinking. You should all just stay away from me. I'm bad news, okay?"

"Hey," I begin. "We've all made mistakes here. Sometimes we've even made them on purpose. But usually there's a reason. When you did that to us, it felt like you were really trying to get us. It hurt."

"I wasn't trying to hurt you. Honest. I guess I was just trying to get your attention, hoping you'd think I was funny." She pauses now, as if she's thinking. "Or maybe I was trying to get my dad's attention. I don't know. Ever since he and my mom split up, it's like I don't exist anymore. He's too busy with his new life now."

"Hey, I know how that feels," says Allie. "My dad's like totally checked out on us."

Marissa looks at Allie now. "Really?"

Just then the warning bell rings.

"Well, before we split up," says Laura quickly. "You need to know something else."

Now Marissa looks as if she's ready to cry again. "What?"

"We all forgive you."

"Yeah," says Allie, sounding sincere. "No hard feelings."

"That's right," I add. "But for your sake, we really hope you don't ever do something like that again."

She sighs. "I wish I could promise that I won't. But like I said, I'm known for doing stupid stuff without thinking. My mom says I'm too impulsive." Then she studies us for a few seconds. "Thanks for being so nice, you guys. I know I don't deserve this." Then she stands and leaves.

"That was pretty cool," says Cesar as he picks up his tray.

Jake says nothing, just sits there twisting on his lip ring as if he's trying to figure us all out. And I admit we are quite an act to take in. Not that we're acting, I mean. It's just that I'm sure he thought it was all pretty weird. Maybe we provided a good distraction to his own problems.

Then we all head off to class.

Well, that was yesterday, and I didn't see Marissa around at all today. I felt bad about that too. I wanted to reassure her that we're still okay with her. I have a feeling she's still beating herself up about this whole thing. But maybe that's good. Maybe she needs to feel bad and really think about what she did and how her impulsive choices can hurt people—including herself. Anyway, I'm really praying for her. And Allie is too. As for Laura, well, I'm pretty sure her head's in the clouds right now. Hopefully, she had a good time at the prom. As for me, I may go some year—maybe—for now I'd just as soon pass.

BEST DANCE
i'd rather dance with You, God
i'd rather sing Your song
i'd rather be Your girl, God
to You, Lord, i belong
You are my first love
i'm nothing without You
my life, my breath, my song, Lord
i'd rather dance with You
cm

Saturday, May 24

To our amazement, Laura actually made it to practice today—on time. We thought she'd be exhausted after her big night out. And in her defense, she hardly spoke of it at all, other than to say she had a great time and that Ryan is totally wonderful. I really respect her for that. Then we got right down to business and practiced until we were all exhausted. But the Memorial Day concert is on Monday, and we want it to be good—really good. This will be the first big thing we've done since the Battle of the Bands, and there'll be no barfing on guitars before performing this time (so Allie assured us).

After we finished, we sat down and prayed together. Now, I'd like to say we do this every time we practice, but the truth is we don't. And it's not as if I'm saying we should, exactly. But it's sure good when we do. We prayed for the upcoming concert as well as the kids at school who are having troubles (like Marissa and Jake and Spencer) and all the other kids who've made, or seem interested in making, commitments to God.

Also, we decided it wouldn't hurt to make some last-minute posters to place at school to announce the memorial concert. I don't know why we didn't think of this sooner since the kids from McFadden (that come to youth group) have been doing this already, and the local Christian radio station has been advertising it too. But it was Allie's idea, and since she's the artist, we put her in charge. She's going to draw up some posters, then ask Greg if we can decorate them during youth group tomorrow. I'm sure he won't mind.

I'm really looking forward to Monday since my brother Josh and (I think) Caitlin are both coming to hear us perform. It'll be so cool to see them again. I'm also pretty curious to see how the two of them interact with each other. I haven't seen them actually together since their breakup last winter. Although Caitlin assured me on the phone this week that they really do speak to each other now. "Just as friends though," she said, as if to clarify. "That's what we need to be to each other for the time being."

"For the time being?" I asked hopefully.

She laughed. "Yeah, I'm sticking to that one-day-at-a-time thing. It's a lot easier than trying to predict the future."

"That's cool."

Still, if I were to predict the future, I'd guess that those two will eventually end up together, permanently. But I suppose I could be wrong. Nah!

Anyway, this girl-guy talk makes me think of Cesar. I know I haven't written much about him, or rather my feelings about him, but I have to admit I really think he's cool. Not just to look at either. But here's what's ironic...ever since he invited God into his life, he doesn't seem nearly as interested in me as he used to be. Before, he would say things, or hint at things, that made me think he liked me—like he wanted to date me. Now he acts more like a brother or just a good buddy. And that's cool, I guess. But suddenly I'm thinking: I really wish he'd ask me out. Now how weird is that? Maybe I just have spring fever.

Better to forget such nonsense (not that Cesar is nonsense—he's definitely not). But I think I need to focus more on my music—and God, of course!

KEEPING MY HEART ON YOU
keeping my mind on You
i'm holding on tight

to what i know's true
all through the night
keeping my eyes on You
i follow Your lead
You'll see me through
give me what i need
keeping my heart on You
i'm hanging on fast
to Your mercies new
Your love that'll last
keeping my heart on You
cm

Eleven

Monday, May 26

Totally rad night! <u>The best!!!</u> And I'm not just talking about our performance either. The evening started out with some college kids (most of them used to go to McFadden) sharing about how the shooting at their high school had impacted their lives during the past two years. Even Josh and Caitlin got up to share—a complete surprise to me since I thought they'd come all this way just to hear us perform. But what they said was really cool and I think it touched the crowd.

About ten kids shared altogether, including Caitlin's good friend Beanie Jacobs (I think I liked what she said the best), but it was interesting to hear how each person had been touched in a completely different way. And as Caitlin said, there's no way of knowing how far a life like Clay's might reach. And I can personally attest to that since it was at his very gravestone where I found God. I still get blown away when I think of what happened that day. I even shared a little bit about it—very briefly—before we started to play.

And it felt <u>so good</u> to be back together again

as a band (without Willy stepping in for Laura—although we still tease him about that). And I think we sounded pretty hot too—if I do say so myself. Obviously, I wouldn't say this in public, it would sound annoyingly arrogant, but I can say it in the privacy of my diary. We were really, really on fire tonight!!! It's like it all just came together, better than any practice we've ever had. Better than when we made our CD. Way better than the Battle of the Bands—and there was no barfing tonight. It's like we really connected and then we got energized by the crowd. Their reaction to our music was unbelievable! I had in no way expected them to be so responsive. It was very cool. I still get goose bumps to think about it. We did an encore. Fortunately, we had a song all planned. (Okay, we had a feeling it could happen—or at least we hoped it would.)

Then after we finished, Pastor Tony spoke for a bit. He didn't talk for long, but what he said was straight from the heart. He even got a little teary eyed when he read a letter that Clay had written to him a few months before the shooting. I'm pretty sure at least half the audience was in tears by the time he finished. Then he invited Redemption back up, and we played this song that he'd asked us to end with. It's a song Clay wrote before he was killed. We could barely keep from choking up while we sang. Really powerful lyrics.

CLAY'S SONG

Worthless, useless, piece of trash
My life was ruined in a flash
Strung out, hung out, left for dead
Till I heard what Jesus said:
"I'm the truth, the life, the way
Listen to the words I say,
Only I can set you free
To reach God, come through Me."
So I fell down on my knees
Here's my life, Lord, take it please.
Worthless, useless, piece of trash—
God redeemed me in a flash!
Strung out, hung out, Jesus died
On a cross, He sanctified
On His head He took my sin
Just to make me clean again
Life will never be the same
God has given me His name
Everything and all I do
My Lord, I give my all to you.

Then Greg, our youth pastor, came up and
invited people who wanted to show that they were
committing or recommitting their lives to Christ
to raise their hands. Now, I know we were supposed to have our heads bowed and not looking
around, but I couldn't help myself, plus I had a
good vantage point up on the stage. But in a way I

was glad that I did because it looked like nearly
everyone raised their hands. It was totally
amazing.

Now here's the best part of the whole night—
even better than how fantastic it felt to play to a
crowd who by all appearances loved us. Among the
kids at the concert (and a lot of them were friends
from school) I had spotted Marissa and Jake
standing with Cesar, and I'm guessing he brought
them. AND when Greg made his invitation, all
three of them raised their hands.

Now, I'm not positive this really means something. It's entirely possible they were just react-
ing to peer pressure and didn't want to feel left
out for being the only ones not responding. Only
God knows for sure. But I am believing they meant
it. And I'm praying for all of them—that they'll
take it seriously.

It's funny though, because not long ago I
really wanted school to be over and done with.
But now, after seeing all these particular kids
raise their hands, I'm not so sure. It makes me
kind of sad to think we've got less than two weeks
left. I guess we'll have to think of some fun
things to do with everyone this summer.
Something to encourage them to hang in there.
Maybe Greg will have some ideas.

I got to talk to Josh and Caitlin for a little
while after the concert. They were both heading

back to their colleges since it's the week before
finals, and it sounds as if they've got a lot of
studying to do. In light of that, I'm really
impressed that they came at all. I couldn't help
but watch them as they spoke to each other. I was
worried they might act kind of stiff and formal,
considering what they went through last winter.
But to my relief they acted like old friends. They
even hugged each other (and me) when it was time
to go. I'm so glad Josh isn't mad about her breaking up with him anymore.

"Can you believe it's been two years since we
lost Clay?" he said to Caitlin.

"In some ways it seems like it happened just a
few weeks ago," she said. "But then it seems like
another lifetime too. We've all changed so much
since then."

Josh nodded. "Yeah, we've all grown up a lot."

She smiled. "Some of us are still growing."

Josh laughed and pointed at himself. "And
some of us still have a long way to go too."

Josh seems changed. It may be my imagination,
but I don't think so. He seems more humble or
quiet or thoughtful. I'm not sure how to describe
it, but it's good. Before, he used to come across as
kind of this know-it-all, but now he seems to
listen more. He seems softer somehow. But not in
a wimpy way. It's hard to explain. But I really
like it. I guess he's just maturing, which I know

sounds silly coming from the "baby" sister. But
there were some years when I absolutely could not
stand my "Mr. Perfect" brother. He could act so
superior sometimes. But now he's different.

And I wonder if Caitlin's breakup has something to do with it. Or maybe not. Caitlin seems
pretty much the same, only older and more mature.
I used to think she was a little shallow sometimes. Okay, shallow's not the right word, because
she's always been sort of deep too. But I used to
compare her to some of the preppy chicks that I
was so mad at. I suppose I even categorized her
with them. I know that was wrong. Still, I think
she's changed too. Maybe it has something to do
with her roommate, Liz Banks. I know those two
have been through a lot this year. But when I
asked, Caitlin said things are going much better
with Liz now.

"She's still searching," Caitlin said. "So keep
praying for her."

"I am. Man, you should see my prayer list these
days."

"Do you pray for every single one of them every
day?" asked Josh. But the way he asked wasn't
like he was checking up on me (like he used to),
but more like he was really interested.

"Actually, I ask God to show me who to pray
for," I said kind of sheepishly. "I'm not sure I
could handle the whole list at once. Then I just

pray for whichever names seem to jump out at me."

"Cool." Josh smiled and put his arm around my shoulders. "You know what, Chloe?"

"What?"

"I am so proud of you."

I smiled. For some reason that meant a lot to me. "Thanks."

"Me too," agreed Caitlin. "And your band is unbelievable." She shook her head dramatically. "I mean it; you guys sound as good as anything I've heard on the radio."

I was getting kind of embarrassed now (well, loving it too). But I thanked her and told her I'd pass her comments on to Laura and Allie. And then they both had to take off. It was hard to see them go—and then I realized they'd be back for summer break! They both have jobs here in town, and they're planning to go to the Mexico orphanage mission at the end of summer—at the same time!!! Maybe I'll see if I can tag along.

SO GOOD
You're so good
so fantastically good
thanks for all You do
to bring us back to You
keep us in Your hand
fill us with Your love
and mercy

and joy
You're so good!
amen

Friday, May 30

I've made a habit not to write too much about
Tiffany Knight in my diary during the past few
months. Not because she's turned into some
wonderful and lovely person, but I guess I
thought it was better not to give her too much
attention, since she was still taking her shots
at me on a fairly regular basis. No more shoving
me against the lockers, but she gets her little
snipes in.

But here's what's weird.

She was nice to me today. "Nice," is that the
right word? Maybe according to Allie's defini-
tion, which would be something like this:
"obnoxiously polite and falsely sweet." Yeah, I
guess that's kind of how she seemed, but I could
be wrong.

Okay, I know that sounds judgmental. But this
is a girl who made my life unbelievably miserable
last fall. A girl who has taken every possible
opportunity to slight me or dis me or even elbow
me in the hallway (always acting like it's an acci-
dent). This is a girl that I have to ask God to help
me forgive almost every time I see her coming—or

seventy times seven. (Since that's how many times Jesus says we need to forgive someone who offends us—it's intended to mean infinity.) And of course Tiffany and her wannabes have offended me so many times that it feels like infinity.

But anyway, today she comes up to me after choir and smiles and says, "Congratulations on your concert, Chloe."

Well, I didn't even say anything at first. Like I was waiting for the next shoe to fall or for her to whack me over the head or to pull the rug out or something else totally mean. But she just stood there, smiling. Now, I hate to say it, but this girl's smile is a scary thing.

"Uh, thanks." I'm sure I was frowning slightly with unbelief. I started to move toward the door, kind of embarrassed that a few other girls were watching us, including Laura who was waiting in the hallway for me with a surprised expression on her face.

"And," Tiffany continued loudly as if to stop me from exiting. "I was hoping we might start to get along better from now on."

Okay, I had to bite my tongue just then. I mean, literally. I could feel my teeth clenching down on the tip of my tongue and it hurt. But I was thinking, "we" could get along better? What's with this "we" business? When have I ever initiated anything the least bit confrontational with her?

She's the one who's acted like a complete moron this whole year. Still, I managed to keep my mouth shut for a few seconds. It must've been a God-thing.

"You do believe in forgiving, don't you, Chloe?"

I nodded, studying her face, trying to see what she was really hoping to accomplish here. Was she serious? "Yeah," I finally said, "forgiving is what Jesus is all about."

"So?"

"Of course." I nodded again, firmly this time, forcing my head to move up and down as if to convince myself too. "I do forgive you."

She smiled again. "Good. I was hoping we could become friends." She glanced toward the hallway. "With Laura too."

I forced a smile to my lips. By now it felt as if everyone in choir was staring at us, not to mention Mr. Thompson, our choir director, who was still standing by the piano, pretending to sort papers. "Yeah, that's cool," I said. "My goal is to be friends with everyone, no matter who they are." I didn't really mean that last bit as a jab, but she could take it however she wanted.

So now I'm wondering, what in the world does this mean? Am I making too much of it? And why does it make me so nervous? I know I should just trust God with the whole stupid thing. But it's a bit unnerving. Laura laughed and said, "Even if

Tiffany is buddying up to us because the popular kids like Cortney and Torrey have been treating us nicely, well, what of it? Just let it go, Chloe. No big deal."

And I suppose it is preferable to being bullied by Tiffany and her steadily shrinking group of wannabes. Still, I guess I don't completely trust her. And the truth is, I don't really want to be friends with her either. Not that I want to be her enemy anymore, or her target either. But FRIENDS??? Give me a break!

On a happier note, it's been interesting talking to Marissa and Jake this week. And this is my take on what happened with them on Monday night. I could be totally loopy, but I think Jake has sincerely made a commitment to God. Cesar agrees with me. But we're still not too sure about Marissa. And yet we don't want to judge her either. But something about her doesn't quite ring true. Allie agrees with us on this too, but Laura says we're wrong. Which is really ironic, if you think about it.

"You guys are starting to act like I did when Pastor Rawlins was always harping at us," Laura said as we carried our trays over to the table where Marissa and the guys were already sitting. Oddly enough, Spencer was there with them today.

"That's not true," said Allie. "But something about Marissa just doesn't feel quite right to me."

"I'm sure she could be <u>close</u> to making a commitment," I continued quickly as we neared the table. "But I don't think—"

"No judging," said Laura in a quiet but stern voice as we drew within earshot.

"Hey, Spencer," I said with a smile. "Long time no see."

He made a half smile or maybe it was a grimace; I'm not sure. "Yeah? Well, I figured I might not be welcome at the goody-goody table anymore. Seems like everyone's going nuts on me here." He shot a look toward Jake.

"Come on, Spence," said Allie lightly. "You are among shoplifters, ex-drug users, witches, and hey, I'll come clean with you—I still smoke a cigarette now and then."

"You do?" I eyed Allie curiously. "You told me you'd stopped."

"I did, mostly." She grinned sheepishly. "But sometimes, I don't know, something comes over me and I just—"

"And I still cuss when I get really mad," admitted Cesar. "I mean, I'm trying to stop, but it's a pretty hard habit to break."

"And I still have these horribly mean thoughts about certain people," I confessed, thinking of Tiffany. "I even had one today. And the Bible says that's as bad as murder."

"Who?" asked Spencer with raised brows. "Who

do you have those thoughts about?"

"I can't say." I made a smirky face at him. "I'm only telling you this so that you'll feel more comfortable with us—we're not goody-goodies. We're no different from you—"

"Except for Jesus," added Laura.

"And He accepts us just as we are," added Allie. "And He's the one who helps us to change."

Marissa sighed. "Well, I feel a little better. I thought maybe we all had to be perfect to get into the club."

Laura laughed. "Yeah, I used to believe that too. But if everyone had to be perfect, who would actually qualify?" Then she told everyone about her plan to have some sort of Bible study or sharing time starting next fall. She asked if they would come.

Spencer groaned. "You gotta be kidding. We used to do that back in grade school. We went to this special release time where we had to listen to all these stupid stories and play these dumb games. It was so lame. You're not going to do something like that, are you?"

"Well, if it was so bad, why'd you go?" asked Allie.

"Just to get out of class and have snacks."

Allie smacked her lips. "Mmm, what kind of snacks?"

We had to laugh.

"Hey, we could have snacks too," offered Laura.

Spencer rolled his eyes. "Yeah? It'd take more than some stupid cookies to get me to come."

I'm sure if we offered a little free grass, he'd be the first there and the last one to leave. But maybe God will help us think of something. It's a ways off anyway. But it's weird; with just a week left of school, things are starting to really happen. And I guess I feel a little sad to see it all end.

GOD HELP US
God, help them
show them Your way
reach out Your hand
hold them today
God, help them
open their eyes
heal their hearts
hear their cries
God, use me
show me Your way
to reach out my hand
and help them today
God, help me
open my eyes
heal my heart
hear my cries.
amen

Twelve

Sunday, June 1

Allie and I were just coming out of youth group today when we were practically tackled by Willy. "Did you hear the news?" he asked as he grabbed us both by the arm. His blue eyes literally flamed with excitement and a wide smile was splayed across his craggy face. Now to fully appreciate this, you'd have to understand how Willy looks sort of ridiculous when he smiles real big since the tooth next to his front tooth is gold, and his bushy mustache is usually trimmed slightly crooked. And come to think of it, he doesn't usually grin like that either. Usually he's pretty cool and laid back—a real mellow seventies kind of dude.

"Huh?" Allie looked slightly stunned as she stared up at his strange expression.

"What's up, Willy?" I asked. "You look like you just got a personal message from God or else won the lottery or something."

He shook his head. "Nope. Not me personally. But maybe you guys did."

"What?" I studied his odd expression and actually wondered if he could possibly be having

some kind of weird flashback trip (from his wild
drug days back before he found God).

"What are you talking about?" demanded Allie.

"Well, come in here." He pulled us into Pastor
Tony's office then closed the door behind us.
"Okay, sit down, both of you, and take a deep
breath."

Without questioning him, we obeyed.

"Now listen." He slowly sat down in Pastor
Tony's big leather chair then leaned forward with
his elbows on the desk. Knowing Pastor Tony, I
figured this was probably okay. "You see," he
began slowly, as if planning his words. "I have
this old friend from the music business. Well,
he's retired now, but he has a younger friend
who's still in the recording industry—and his
name is Eric Green. He's a Christian and is pretty
high up in Omega—a Christian recording company.
Anyway, I sent him your demo CD a while back
and..." Willy started tapping his fingers
together and grinning just like the Cheshire cat.

"Cool," said Allie. "Did he like it?"

"Better than that." He kept tapping his fingers together, only faster now, but his eyes were
on fire.

"What?" I demanded with a seriously pounding
heart. I'm sure my blood pressure was getting
high as well. "What in the world are you trying to
tell us, Willy?"

"Well..." He actually snickered now, as if he almost couldn't contain himself any longer. "You have no idea how hard this has been for me. Trying not to spill the beans about this whole thing, but Eric called me last weekend and told me he really liked the demo and that he wanted to see and hear you girls in person. So I told him about the memorial concert, and—"

"A record producer actually came to our concert?" I was standing now, leaning forward and peering at Willy.

He nodded. "And man, was he ever impressed."

"You're kidding?!?" Allie stood up too. "A real, honest-to-goodness, legitimate record company?"

He nodded again.

"What does this mean?" I asked, and I could hear the tremor of excitement in my voice. This is just way too good to be true.

Now honestly, about now it looked as if Willy's face was about to explode with all this previously contained delight. "Well, ladies, I think it means he's going to offer Redemption a recording contract."

Allie and I both screamed. (We were later relieved to see that the door was firmly closed since the morning service had already started.) Well, we both jumped up and down and hugged each other and screamed again and hugged Willy and thanked him over and over.

Then finally after we settled down, I begged him to tell us the whole story again—this time with all the details. Then we took some time to call Allie's mom, who hadn't left for work yet, and my parents, who hadn't gone to their church today. (They only go about once a month or so these days.) I think Allie's mom didn't quite believe her, but Allie said she sounded pretty happy just the same. On the other hand, my mom didn't seem to think it was such a big deal, or else she wasn't taking me seriously. I'll just say it felt a little anticlimactic.

"Have they actually offered you girls a real contract?" she asked. The skepticism in her voice was unmistakable.

"No, but Willy thinks there's a pretty good chance they will."

"But are they a reliable company, Chloe? Or are they expecting you girls to invest your own money? I've heard about those companies that tell you you're going to hit the big times, but then they make you pay your own way. They had an episode on a news show about it. It's a real scam. And you've already nearly depleted your savings on your little band."

The way she said "little band" was the final blow, but I determined not to let her lack of enthusiasm bring me down. "Oh, I'll explain the details later this afternoon, Mom. Just tell Dad the good news and I'll see you." Parents!

Fortunately, Willy's enthusiasm helped make up for my mom's lack of it. And it wasn't Pastor Tony's fault that Allie and I could barely sit still in church. As soon as the service ended, we grabbed Willy and begged him to drive us over to where Laura's church was just getting out. Actually, I think he wanted to do it. Then you should've heard the three of us girls in Laura's church parking lot. I'm sure half the folks in town heard us squealing, including everyone from her church. But it was pretty cool, and when they found out, they all gave us a great big cheer right in the parking lot.

Finally, the crowd began dispersing and Willy hushed us girls down. "Now, let's not lose our heads just yet, because it's still not 100 percent for sure. These things never are, not until the ink from the signatures is dry."

"What's the next step?" asked Laura's dad. It seemed as if he was getting into this, although her mom still looked a little reserved.

"Yeah," I asked. "What do we do from here?"

"Eric wants to fly you girls out to Nashville as soon as school is out. You can each bring one parent or guardian with you. Then you'll do an official audition in the recording studio, in front of the powers that be. After that they'll have a meeting and decide whether they want you or not."

"Do you think we really have a chance?" asked Allie. And I could clearly see the hopes of fame and fortune gleaming in her eyes. She's always wanted to be rich and famous. I just hope this doesn't go to her head.

"You know, I think we should put this whole thing into God's hands," said Willy in a sober voice. He looked around at the small crowd of us gathered next to the Mitchell's car—we three girls and Laura's parents and James. "Why don't we pray right now?"

And so we did. And to pray like that, out there in the June sunshine, felt like a huge sigh of relief to me. It felt as if the weight was suddenly lifted as we put the whole thing into God's hands. "Your will be done," Willy finally said. And we all said, "Amen!"

Then Willy offered to take Allie and me home and speak with both of our parents. "Thanks," said Allie. "My mom acted all happy and everything, but she kinda sounded like she thought I was making it all up too. Like when I was a little girl and I got my hopes up that I was going to win this dirt bike in a drawing at the hardware store in town. Of course, I didn't win. Anyway, it'll probably help to have her hear about it from a grown-up."

So I waited at Allie's as Willy explained to Elise what exactly was going on. And it was really sweet to see little Davie climb onto Willy's

knee as he spoke. Davie sat there quietly playing
with Willy's cross (Willy always wears this cross
made from two nails hanging by a leather cord),
and every once in a while Davie would reach up
and pat Willy on the cheek and just smile.

"Well, I guess that sounds legit." Elise stood
and shook her head as if it was all just sinking
in. "Amazing though. I'm sorry, I don't mean to
rush you off, but I really have to be to work in
about fifteen minutes."

"No problem." Willy set Davie on the floor,
then ruffled his hair.

"And I hope they don't expect me to pay for
Allie's plane tickets or hotel room or anything."
She frowned as she picked up her work smock and
purse. "We're barely scraping by as it is."

He waved his hand. "No, no, you won't need to
worry about a thing. The recording company will
provide two round-trip tickets as well as food
and hotel rooms and any other expenses for each
girl along with one adult to accompany her."

Elise looked startled now. "Well, I can't possibly go to Nashville with her. I have work—and I
have Davie—and I—"

"Mom!" cried Allie. "You have to go."

"It sounds fun, Allie, but you know as well as
I do that it's impossible." Elise frantically dug
in her purse for her car keys. "Maybe you should
ask your father to—"

"No way!" Allie shook her head. "He's the last person on—"

"I'm sorry, but I don't have time for this right now. We'll just have to figure it out later."

Allie looked a little bummed now, but Willy assured her that it would all work out. "If it's God's will, you don't need to worry about a thing. It'll all fall right into place."

Next we went to my house, but by the time we got there my parents had already left. A note on the breakfast bar said they were off playing golf with the Stephensens until four.

"Sorry, Willy," I said as I walked him back to the door. Now I felt a little let down too. Here I am having the biggest event of my life and my parents take off. But then why should that surprise me?

Willy turned and looked at me. "You should call Josh."

"Yes!" I nodded eagerly. "That's what I'll do."

And so I called and actually got Josh, live, on the phone. He'd just gotten back from church and was changing his clothes to go jogging. He was so excited that he totally made up for Mom's lack of enthusiasm. He whooped and hollered and even told his roommate that his little sister was going to be famous.

Then I told him about Mom's reaction.

"Oh, you know how she can be, Chloe. Don't take it to heart. It's probably from working at the law firm too long. She thinks everyone's a rip-off artist." We both laughed.

And so, despite Mom's ho-hum attitude, I am still excited. I think something big is in the works. And I'm not going to worry because, like Willy said, it's all in God's hands. If He wants it to happen, it will. If not, well, we'll have to accept that as His will too. But just the same, I really, really want it to happen. I've never felt more alive or more in love with God than that night we did the memorial concert. It's like everything in me was connected that night. It was so right on!

RIGHT ON, GOD
life with You
is so right on
connected
aligned
on target
in sync
together
with-it
bull's-eye
totally jived
right on, God
You are so right on!
amen

Monday, June 2

Willy came over to talk to my parents tonight. I can already see that my dad's getting pretty excited about the whole thing, especially after talking about it to his friend Ron Stephensen (a music professor at the college who's always believed in Redemption's possibilities), but for whatever reason, my mom's still holding back.

"This is quite an opportunity," said Willy after he explained the basic deal to my parents. "No guarantees, but the experience itself is invaluable and could lead to something else."

"And the music company is paying for every-thing?" my mom asked for what seemed like the sixth time.

Willy nodded. "You bet. Eric Green thinks these girls have the right stuff. And he's fairly high up there at Omega. Still, it's a joint decision, and the president has the final say."

"Let's say that Omega does like the band," continued my mom. "What does that really mean? What kind of a contract are we talking about? Is it really worth all this fuss?"

"Do you know much about the music industry, Mrs. Miller?"

She smiled politely. "You can call me Joy."

"Joy." He smiled back. "Do you know much about the industry?"

She shook her head.

"Well, the girls won't be instant millionaires, but it's not peanuts either."

"It's all a little overwhelming," said my dad, then he grinned. "But if Chloe can handle it, then I suppose we can too."

"Like I said—" Willy shook his head as if still taking it in himself—"it's an amazing opportunity. And even though the odds are still stacked against them for making it <u>really</u> big, those odds are still a whole lot better than winning the lottery."

"So, who wants to go to Nashville with me?" I asked.

Mom frowned. "That's not a very good week for me to be gone from work, Chloe. There's a big case and—"

"No problem," said Dad. "I'd <u>love</u> to go!"

"Really?"

He nodded. "School's out next week. And I've got vacation time."

"What exactly do you do, Stan?" asked Willy. "I know you work at the local college."

"He's the dean of admissions," I said proudly.

"It's not as if I have the whole summer off, but I can certainly take some vacation time off for this."

"Thanks, Dad."

"Thank <u>you</u>, Chloe." He reached over and

squeezed my shoulder. "I'm looking forward to it."

And for the first time since I scored the winning soccer goal back in seventh grade, it felt
like Dad was actually proud of me. Really proud.
And that was so cool. Still, I can't figure Mom.
It's as though she's not even excited. It almost
feels as if she'd like the whole thing to just blow
over. It's weird.

LESS THAN PERFECT
life's not supposed to be perfect
i know this
there's always something...
like your cool new shoes
wear a blister on your toe
or your bike has a flat
when you're ready to go
or you get a big zit
before your first date
or fall on your face
after doing something great
there's always something
i know this
i just wish that sometimes
everything would be perfect
cm

Thirteen

Thursday, June 5

It's funny. Last week I didn't really want school to end. But then we learned about this recording thing, and suddenly it's like I can't get out of there quick enough. Like adios, amigos, see ya in September! Just the same, I did really make an effort to stay connected to my friends and not appear as if I was overly eager to just blow the joint. Even though I was.

It's amazing how fast the word spread about our audition. Thanks to Allie, I'm sure. Not that I blame her exactly. And not that I even mind. It was actually kind of fun having kids treat us like celebrities.

"You guys are <u>so</u> lucky," said Torrey as we were leaving choir today.

"Yeah." Cortney made a face. "You'll probably get so rich and famous that you won't even remember the little people anymore."

I had to laugh at that—"the little people"—everyone knows that Torrey and Cortney are at the top of the Harrison High food chain, at least in our class. And even though there was a time I could barely stand them as well as their somewhat preppy ways, I must admit I kind of like their attention now. And this bothers me a little. But I could tell that Laura and Allie liked the attention too.

"It's not a done deal," Laura reminded them. "It's just an audition. The recording company might hate us."

"Or Allie might barf on my guitar."

The girls standing around us laughed. "Did she really do that?" asked Torrey.

I nodded.

"That must've really stunk," said someone from behind us. I turned to see Tiffany and a couple of her friends listening.

"Yeah, it did." I glanced at Laura. "Speaking of Allie, didn't we say we'd meet her for lunch?"

Cortney patted us both on the backs. "Well, you guys stay in touch. Let us know how it goes. We want to be the first to hear if we know someone who's becoming famous."

I laughed. "Even if we do get a record deal, that hardly means we'll be famous."

"Around here it does," said Torrey. "Nothing like this ever happens around here."

"Tell you guys what," I said as Laura and I moved toward the door. "If we actually sign a contract, we'll do a special gig at the Paradiso to celebrate. I'm sure Mike won't mind."

"Cool," said Cortney. "Let us know."

"Yeah," said Tiffany from behind her. "Let me know too."

I nodded. "Yeah, or maybe you'll just see us on MTV."

This made them laugh, then Laura and I started heading to the cafeteria. Since it was the last day of school, Allie and I wanted to sit with Cesar and the others, but Laura really felt she needed to sit with her old friends.

"It's okay," Allie assured her. "We'll be spending plenty of time together in practice next week and then off to Nashville."

"Yeah, and LaDonna got seriously mad at me yesterday," Laura explained. "She keeps saying I'm going to leave them all behind now that we're almost <u>famous</u>."

"Yeah, that's what Spencer's been saying too," said Allie. "It's like suddenly he's our <u>best</u> friend."

"And when I think of the bad time he's given me over the year..." I said. "Then again, he was the first one at high school who actually tried to be friendly to me," I lowered my voice, "even if it was to offer me a hit."

Now I'm thinking it's funny how "friends" start getting really chummy when it looks as if you're coming into something big. I'm starting to understand how people might feel when they win a bunch of money. Suddenly everyone's your new or old best friend. And it's confusing. How can you be sure who's sincere and who's not? And even though Torrey and Cortney have been nice to me lately, they pretty much thought I was invisible when school first started last fall.

But the fact is, I used to hang with them as well as my old friend Jessie back in middle school. And all three of them dumped me just when I needed them the most. I guess I've mostly forgiven them for that. But then there's Tiffany. After everything that girl's put me through, she's suddenly acting as if it's all hunky-dory between us, as if nothing was ever wrong. And I know I <u>said</u> I forgave her. And God knows I've tried to forgive her a bazillion times. But sometimes I just don't feel like it. And I <u>really</u> don't feel like being her "friend"—ever! For that reason alone, I am so relieved that school is over.

GROW UP
help me to grow up
to move on
to forgive and forget
to be more like You
help me to love others
despite their flaws
and not to judge
lest i become
just like them
amen

Friday, June 6

First official day of summer break. Ahhhh. I slept in until ten, then dropped by the Paradiso to say hi to Mike as well as tell him we might need to postpone our next gig since it looks as if we'll be in Nashville that week.

"Yeah, I heard the news."

"You're kidding? You already heard?"

He nodded as he wiped down the counter. "Jill heard it at the grocery store a few days ago. Don't you know that Redemption is the talk of the town right now?"

I laughed. "Well, this week anyway. We'll see what they say when we come back."

"It's too bad too." He sighed loudly.

"Too bad?"

"Yeah, I was going to offer you a job for the summer."

"Really?"

"Yep. I need someone to help out around here."

"That'd be cool, Mike." I considered this briefly. "And if I was going to work, I can't think of anyplace I'd rather be. But right now I feel like I should focus on my music more."

He looked me in the eyes. "So do I, Chloe. I'm just giving you a bad time. The fact is, I wouldn't even let you work for me. It'd be morally wrong."

I laughed. "Well, I don't know about that."

Then I thought of something. "Allie says she still wants to get a job this summer."

"Isn't she going to be pretty busy too?"

"It's hard to say. We don't really know what's going to happen after the audition. They might just send us packing, and it could be business as usual after we get home from Nashville."

He brightened. "Then, by all means, tell Allie to drop by and see me."

"So we're okay to reschedule the gig for after we get back?"

He grinned. "You're on. We can use the business since the coffee business seems to diminish a little in summertime. Hopefully, it'll be a celebration night."

"Or else a consolation concert."

"If anything big happens, why don't you guys call me from Nashville? We'll put something in the paper about it, and that way we'll get a little free publicity for the Paradiso at the same time."

"Right on."

So I called Allie tonight and told her about the job.

"That'd be cool," she said. "Guess what?"

"Let's see..." Allie knows I hate this game, but I tried to be a good sport. "Hollywood just called and offered you a movie deal?"

"Yeah, you bet. No, Willy offered to go to Nashville in place of Mom."

"Really?"

"Yeah, first he offered to babysit Davie so Mom could come with me, but she said she couldn't afford to miss that much work."

"That was sweet of him."

"Yeah, he's so cool." She lowered her voice. "I think Mom thinks so too."

"Really?"

"Yeah, but don't breathe a word to anyone—I mean it."

"Speaking of Willy," I continued on a new note. "I was wondering if he'd be interested in acting as our manager. I realize he's got his plumbing business to take care of and everything, but he knows so much about music and he's been so helpful already. What do you think?"

"I think it makes perfect sense. But we better talk to Laura first."

"I'll ask my dad what he thinks too."

"Is your mom still acting weird about it?"

"Yeah. I don't get her. She acts almost as if there's nothing unusual going on in my life. Like deals like this happen to everyone, all the time. I'm so thankful that Dad's excited."

"Yeah. He's cool."

"Did you tell your dad yet?"

She groaned. "Don't remind me. What a mistake."

"What'd he say?"

"Oh yeah, he was excited all right. It's like I could imagine these dollar signs flashing in his eyes—like he's thinking, 'Hey, my little girl's gonna make me a rich man.'"

"That's too bad."

"Yeah, and he was acting like he wants to go to Nashville with me. That was before Willy offered. I still haven't even told him. The truth is, I don't want him along. I mean, how do you tell your dad that you don't want him? And besides, shouldn't he just know that? It's not as if he's done anything to help us out lately. He misses most of his child support checks lately, and Mom's threatening to take him to court and have them garnish his wages."

I swallowed. It's always hard to know how to respond to things about this guy. On one hand, he is Allie's own flesh and blood. But on the other hand, he's like the scum of the earth.

She sighed. "I guess I better just tell him about Willy, maybe say it's because he's managing us too."

"Yeah, I hope that doesn't make him too mad."

"Well, you know what? I kinda hope it does make him mad. It's like he's gotten away with so much crud anyway. He's hurt my mom so many times. Maybe it's time for him to get his."

"But you probably shouldn't be the one to dish it out, Al."

She grew quiet on the other end.

"Remember last week when Tony taught about how God needs to be the One to make things right in our lives?" I began slowly, not really wanting to preach at her. "He said how things get messed up when we take them into our own hands, instead of asking God to take care of them."

"Yeah, I remember. And he's probably right. Besides, I don't really want to waste my energy on having some big old conflict with Dad right now. I've got lots better things to do."

"That's cool."

After I hung up, I prayed about Allie and the situation with her dad. Even though I think he's a total creep, I don't want to see Allie become bitter toward him. Hopefully, she'll handle it okay. I'm sure she will.

Speaking of parents, I then decided to search out my own. So I found them sitting comfortably in the family room. "Dad, what do you think about Willy managing us?"

Mom's sitting on the couch next to him, her feet daintily tucked beneath her, reading a hardback novel—an Oprah pick, I think. But I can tell by her expression that she's listening very carefully to this conversation.

My dad just smiled and said, "I think that's a great idea, Chloe. He seems to know a lot about the music business."

My mom marked her place and set her book aside. "But what do we really know about him?"

I was a little surprised to hear her actually say something since she acts fairly uninterested, not to mention unimpressed, by this whole thing. "Well, he's been a good friend to us girls," I said in Willy's defense. "And he's given Allie free drumming lessons, plus he's helped arrange a bunch of my songs, and with the CD, and the Battle of the Bands, and, well, a zillion other little things."

"Makes perfect sense to me," said Dad. "And Ron Stephensen seemed impressed with him too."

Mom shook her head. "I'm not so sure. A manager gets a cut, you know? How much do you think he'll take—10, maybe 15 percent? And then I'm assuming the rest will be split three ways."

I shrugged and looked at Dad. "I guess I haven't really given the money side of this whole thing that much thought." Frankly I felt surprised that Mom had. After all, she's the one who's been putting down the whole idea from the start.

"We'll have to cross that bridge when we get there, Joy." My dad folded his paper and picked up the remote. "I think having Willy along will probably be helpful when we're in Nashville, Chloe."

"I think the girls need a lawyer." My mom stood and started pacing. "I know that sounds a little expensive to start with, but you're always hearing about kids getting ripped off in the entertainment industry. We don't want that to happen to the girls."

I studied her furrowed brow as she paced back and forth, trying to figure this woman out. "So, Mom," I finally said, "are you saying that you believe Redemption has a chance to make it—that we might actually get a record contract?"

She looked over at me with a slightly bewildered expression. "Oh, of course, honey. I realize you girls are pretty good...and that it <u>could</u> happen. I'm just not sure that it's going to be worth all the fuss in the end."

Okay, I tried not to take offense at her "pretty good" description, although it sounded to me as if she meant: "pretty good for a bunch of silly kids." I glanced at my dad for some support here.

He frowned slightly. "You're not making complete sense, Joy. If you don't think it's worth all the fuss, then why are you suggesting the girls might need a lawyer?"

"Well, you never know."

Trying hard to fight off my exasperation I took in a deep breath. "So, Mom, tell me, how do you <u>really</u> feel about Redemption? It seems like you don't take us very seriously. Like you don't really believe in us or our talent."

She stopped pacing and looked at me. "That's

not it at all, Chloe."

I could feel her eyes on me, scrutinizing me, as she took in my hair (I recently put a magenta rinse on it, and it has this great sort of purplish brown look) and my piercings and my frayed and holey blue jeans. Even my faded T-shirt was inside out—something she really hated.

"Oh, I get it." I nodded with realization. "You'd like to change our image."

She smiled, as if I were actually offering to let her dress us up in cute little matching outfits—kind of like the Supremes back in the sixties. I glanced uncomfortably at Dad again and thought, "Okay, here's your chance to back me up." And to my amazement he did. "Hey, Joy, you need to get enlightened. Watch some of the other bands out there. Honestly, I saw a couple of groups on MTV that make Redemption look like nice little prep school girls."

"Thanks a lot, Dad." I sank into the couch. Why on earth had God given me parents like this?

"But it's so—" Mom stopped herself, like she was about to say something really mean. "It's so sort of trashy looking, Chloe. Can't you at least wear something that isn't so—well, so old and worn looking?"

"It's called urban, Mom. To me it feels honest and creative, and I happen to like it. Besides, it's comfortable."

"But what about the recording company in Nashville?" she said. "Won't they be expecting something more—more professional looking?"

Fortunately, this made me laugh. "Mom, maybe Dad's right. Maybe you should watch a little MTV. You might begin to understand that the music industry probably expects us to look like this."

Dad laughed too. "Yeah, honey, it's like you're stuck in some kind of time warp here. What do you think bands are supposed to look like these days?"

She shrugged. "Oh, I don't know. I guess I just don't like seeing my little girl looking like such a bum all the time."

I nodded, then to my surprise, I went over and patted her on the back. "It's okay, Mom," I said in a gentle voice. Okay, I was being a little sarcastic too. "I'm sure you love me despite my less-than-tidy appearance."

She sighed in exasperation as if she'd lost the battle. "Of course I love you, Chloe. You're my daughter."

"Okay, then." I turned to Dad. "Maybe you guys should watch a little MTV. I've got a song I want to work on."

And that was that. I left the room and I could still hear their voices, quietly bickering back and forth, and slowly getting louder. My dad sounded like he was standing up for me again.

And even though that felt partly good, another part of me felt incredibly guilty, as if it was my fault they're disagreeing. I mean, there they were sitting together so nice and compatible, then I came in, and, well, there you go.

Honestly, the last thing I want to do right now is to come between them and cause a stupid fight. My parents haven't fought too much since the days when Caleb was at home. They used to fight almost constantly then. In fact, it's still a pretty sore subject with them. And I just don't want to be the one to do that to them all over again.

HELP
o God, help them
through this
i know i'm not an easy kid
but i am what i am
and i am theirs
like it or not
they're stuck with me
but i don't want to
drive them apart
help them
through this
and while You're at it
help me too
amen

Fourteen

Monday, June 9

Allie called me this morning to let me know she got the job at the Paradiso. Mike's letting her work a split shift, a few hours in the morning and a few in the evening, so Allie can still attend band practice in between. He said music comes first.

I had just hung up with Allie when Cesar called me. He said he had the day off and asked if I wanted to go on a bike ride with him. I told him I had to be back by one to practice. And he said that was cool and so off we went.

Okay, now here's what's kind of weird—or ironic—or just plain bizarre. We're on this bike ride, and I'm pretty much letting him lead the way because he says he has this route that he usually takes, and it's a pretty decent workout. But guess where we end up? <u>At the cemetery.</u>

But not the one I usually go to. No, we end up at one on the other side of town, just outside of the city limits. And suddenly I realize that the last time I was here was for Jewel's funeral—almost exactly a year ago. And it's kind of eerie. Not scary exactly, but odd in a Twilight Zone kind of way—the sort of thing that gives you goose bumps.

We park our bikes, and I take a long swig from my water bottle. I feel hot and sweaty, and it was harder than I expected trying to keep up with Cesar. He's in <u>good</u> shape. But after I catch my breath I ask him, "Did you know Jewel Garcia by any chance?"

He looks at me in surprise. "Yeah, she was my cousin."

"You're kidding? Your cousin? That is too weird."

"Why?"

I just shake my head.

"Did you know her too?"

"Not really well. I met her through Caitlin. We used to go visit her in the hospital."

"Is Caitlin that pretty blond girl who was so into religion?"

"Religion?" I look at him funny.

He smiles. "Yeah, it sounds weird to say that now, but that's probably how it seemed to me at the time. Just the same, my aunt, Jewel's mom, really liked her and was glad she visited so much." He studies me now. "But you actually went with her to visit Jewel? Man, I can't even imagine that."

I shake my head at the strange memory. It seems like such a long time ago now—another lifetime. "Yeah, it seems pretty weird to me too, now that I think about it. I don't even know why

Caitlin invited me to go with her in the first place. I guess she thought it'd be good for me to see someone who was a lot worse off than I was."

"You weren't doing too good?"

And then, to my complete and utter amazement, I tell Cesar the whole embarrassing story (without mentioning the guy's name, of course) about how I was hurt by this stupid boy (the "most popular" guy in middle school) who pretended to be my boyfriend in hopes that he could sleep with me, but then tossed me aside when I refused him. I even tell him how all my friends acted after this boy spread his vicious lies.

"It's like I ceased to exist," I finish my story with a wave of my hand. "Poof! Now you see her, now you don't."

"That guy was a total jerk." Cesar snaps the lid back onto his water bottle, then lets a cuss word fly. "I'm sorry, Chloe." He shakes his head. "Just when I think I've used my last foul word another one slips out."

"Hey, it's okay. We're not perfect, you know. And under the circumstances I don't really mind." I smile at him. "In fact, I used to call him every bad name in the book. I think I even made up a few too. I guess that's when I started turning into a pretty tough chick." I laugh.

"Sometimes people act tough so they don't get hurt."

I nod. "Yeah. I know."

Cesar glances over to where a big oak tree is casting its giant shadow over the grass. "I came up here just last week—exactly one year since Jewel died."

"I'd like to see her grave."

"Let's go."

So we silently walk over there, and now I'm thinking about those visits with Jewel in the hospital. I'm remembering how childlike she was with the brain injury from the bullet, and how she loved to sing "Jesus Loves Me." And to my surprise I'm starting to cry, but I'm hoping Cesar won't notice. I don't want to make him feel any worse. I wipe my cheeks with my palms then shove my hands into my pockets as we stand by her grave. The stone is small and square with only her name and the dates. But as I read the stone I'm reminded afresh of how she was only seventeen.

I take in a deep breath then slowly exhale. "What a sad waste—to end it all at seventeen."

"Yeah. I'll be seventeen next fall. It's like life is just beginning."

"I really believe she's in heaven now, but I wonder if she might regret what she did—you know, looking back."

"She was always this really happy person too." Cesar sighed. "She loved to play practical jokes and sing along to the radio. Her favorite drink was Dr Pepper with a lemon wedge. I didn't even believe it when my mom told me what had happened. I really thought she must've gotten Jewel confused with someone else. It didn't make any sense."

"Maybe not to you. But at the time I thought I kind of understood how Jewel might have felt. I guess it sounds stupid now. I mean, what guy is worth killing yourself for? But hey, I'd just had my heart broken by a stupid boy—" I look at Cesar quickly. "Sorry, I didn't mean to imply that all guys are like that or anything."

"Yeah." He nodded. "You know, girls can break hearts too."

So we stand there a little longer, just silently, thinking our own private thoughts, I suppose. And I must admit mine are turning into sort of a jumble by now. But then I realize it's time for me to start heading back.

"I better get going. Laura and Al will kill me if I'm late, especially since I'm the one always harping on them to be on time."

So we race back to my house, getting there just five minutes before one. "I might have time—to grab a shower," I breathlessly tell him as I park my bike. "Thanks for inviting me today."

"Thanks for coming."

We wave good-bye and I dash for the shower.

And while I'm showering I think, "Cesar is really special." And if I wanted a boyfriend I couldn't do any better than someone like him. Even now I get a warm feeling just thinking of him.

I am barely out of the shower when Laura and Allie show up. And we have a really good practice today—about four hours straight. I didn't mention my bike ride with Cesar to them. It's not as though it was a real date or anything. And I seriously doubt that we'll ever be more than just friends. I think even if I wanted it to be more, and maybe I do, it still probably wouldn't happen. Cesar seems kind of reserved, like he's sort of holding me at arm's length now, which is probably a good thing. And now I'm telling myself, "Cesar is cool, but I need to keep him on the back burner for now too." Yet even as I write this, I find myself thinking about him more than ever before.

What would Caitlin think if she knew? Speaking of Caitlin, I think she was supposed to get back in town today. And Josh gets home tomorrow. Thank God I have plenty of distractions in my life—to keep me from going over the edge for Cesar.

I'M HOOKED
eyes on You
the whole way through
it's my choice
to hear Your voice

hold my hand
help me stand
on my feet
and take the heat
for saying no
i won't let go
to You, Lord
i can't afford
to walk away
help me stay
hooked on You
my whole life through
amen

Thursday, June 12

Caitlin, Beanie, Jenny, and Josh watched us practice tonight. Kind of like a mini concert of sorts.
But we had asked them here to critique us. Of
course, Willy was here too. He's coming to all our
practices this week, but his help is primarily in
the music area. We invited the others to help us
with how we look—our persona and stage presence
and such. To be honest, it was my mom's idea, but
then she got Josh involved, which made it a little
easier for me to handle.

"You guys sound fantastic," said Josh as we
finished. "And that drum set is really cool,
Allie."

She grinned and clanged the cymbal. "Yeah, totally rad."

"Okay." Caitlin stepped forward, glancing at her notes. "You guys ready for this?"

Beanie laughed. "Leave it to Caitlin to make notes."

"I'm just trying to be helpful."

"Go ahead," I told her, bracing myself for criticism.

"Well, first off, you guys should smile more."

"Smile?" I started to protest.

"Let me finish first," she said. "I don't mean you have to look like grinning goons, but you should look like you're enjoying yourselves, and move around more, relax and have fun."

I nodded. "Yeah, you're right about that. And we usually do better on a real stage when we have more space, you know?"

"But when you audition in Nashville, it'll be in a studio," Willy reminded us. "So you better keep that in mind while you're practicing now."

"Right," agreed Allie with a grin. "You guys move around more."

"And you too, Allie. You can loosen up on the drums a little," continued Caitlin. "The next thing is eye contact. You need to make more eye contact with your audience. It looks like you're trying too hard to do the music, like you're not enjoying yourselves."

"You're probably talking to me," said Laura sheepishly. "I sometimes have a problem with this."

"Yeah," said Jenny. "You need to show a lot more confidence. You girls are really good, and you should play like you really believe it."

We were all nodding and I'm sure making mental notes. "You're right," I said. "It's easier in a concert when the crowd is clapping and stuff. But when we're just in a practice room, well, it's different."

Willy pointed his finger in the air. "But in Nashville..."

"Right." Laura turns back to our critique group. "Anything else?"

"Well, I have some thoughts," said Beanie. "I'm curious about what you guys plan to wear when you audition."

I looked down at my faded gray T-shirt (my favorite one) and the torn jeans with safety pins holding them together, and I shrugged. "Probably something like this."

"Yeah," Allie agreed. "We just want to look like our normal selves."

Laura kept silent, but I could guess what she was thinking.

Beanie stood there for a moment, arms folded across her front, studying us. "Hey, I'm all for urban. It's comfy, it's cool. But I still have some thoughts. I don't want to be pushy though."

Now, I have to admit that I've always admired Beanie's style. She is not a bit preppy, and I can tell her clothes have no designer labels, but she always looks very cool. "I want to know what you're thinking," I said.

"Me too," said Allie.

Laura nodded.

Beanie looked from me to Allie. "Well, I think that you could clean up your act a little."

Everyone laughed.

And I had to smile. "So what did you have in mind? Matching sequined dresses? Maybe something in pink?"

Beanie studied us for another long moment, this time rubbing her chin as if in deep contemplation. "I could see you girls in something vintage. Sort of urban cleaned up. And definitely not all alike. It's like you'll all need something that fits your various personalities. For instance, I think Allie might look good in something with a little lace."

"Lace?" Allie giggled.

"And I could see Laura in something colorful and fun, kind of artsy to go with her hair."

Laura smiled. "I could get into that."

Now Beanie was looking at me and frowning. Then it's like a light went on. "Leather. Chloe, you'd look cool in something leather."

"Yeah, that's easy for you to say." The skeptic in me came out. "But how do we go about this? We sure don't have much time."

Beanie grinned. "I'll help."

"You guys better take her up on that offer," said Caitlin quickly.

"Yeah," agreed Jenny. "No one can shop retro like our Beanie."

"And she knows how to sew and alter things too," added Caitlin.

"Really?" Allie was getting excited now. "You'd really help us?"

"We only have four days," said Laura. "Is that enough time?"

Beanie nodded. "If we start first thing tomorrow."

And so it's set. We're going to practice smiling and moving and acting like we're in a real concert. And Beanie's going to be our fashion expert. Worst case scenario is we won't like Beanie's choices and we'll just go with plan A and be ourselves. Still, I'm curious about what Beanie can do.

Allie stayed after everyone else left, and we hung out in my room dreaming about what we're going to do when we make it big.

"We could, you know." Allie stared at her image in my mirror, as if she was imagining herself as some big rock star.

"Or not." I flopped down on my bed and sighed. "It's in God's hands."

She came and sat beside me. "But God could do this, if He wants, you know."

"I know. But sometimes it makes my brain tired to think about it too much."

"Yeah." She nodded. "Sometimes it scares me a little. I mean, for the most part I really, really want it more than anything else. But there's this other little part of me that just wants to be a normal girl—you know? Have a normal family and a normal home and maybe even a normal boyfriend—and be in clubs at school and go on double dates and go to the prom. Of course, that's all impossible." She leaned over and peered at me. "Do you think I'm totally stupid and hopelessly shallow now?"

I laughed. "No." Then I sat up. "In fact, I feel the exact same way sometimes."

She looked stunned. "No way. Not you. Not Chloe Miller, tough chick extraordinaire. You're the rebel, the one who wants to be different and to learn everything the hard way."

I shook my head. "Not always." And then for some reason I told her about Cesar and the bike ride.

"I knew it." She punched my pillow with her fist and then groaned as if she were in serious pain.

"You're mad at me?"

"No. But it just figures. First Laura and Ryan hook up. And now you and Cesar." She buried her face in the pillow and pretended to wail. "I'm going to end up the old maid—the only one without a boyfriend!"

"Hang on, Al." I shook her shoulder. "Cesar is NOT my boyfriend."

She looked up at me, then rolled her eyes. "So you say, now."

"I mean it. We're only friends. He has absolutely no interest in anything more—"

"Ha! That's where you're totally wrong, Chloe. Cesar has always had a crush on you."

"No way!"

"Way!"

"How do you know?"

She looked pretty smug now. "He's told me enough times."

"You're nuts."

"No, you're nuts. Especially if you don't like him back. Man, Cesar is the coolest guy. Marissa will be seriously jealous though."

"Have you heard from her lately?"

"No, but she knows we're pretty busy this week. I told her we'd get together with her after Nashville." Allie flopped across on my bed. "Ah, 'Nashville,'" she sighed. "I just love the sound of that word."

After I drove Allie home tonight, I thought about what she'd said about Cesar having a crush on me. All right, I'll admit I used to think he liked me, and he hinted at going out once. Back before he became a Christian. But something seems to have changed since then. And not in a bad way. It's just that he doesn't seem so flirty, and he's more serious. And really, I think he just wants to be friends now. But I guess I could be wrong.

JUST FRIENDS
just friends
it begins
how it ends
no pretense
why more?
close the door
to amour
evermore
i'll adjust
if i must
no more lust
simply trust
what will be
endlessly
i can see
God loves me
cm

Fifteen

Saturday, June 14

This morning when Beanie dropped off the clothes she'd altered for us, I told her that she should think about becoming a fashion designer, and she said she's actually considering it.

"It's funny," she said when we went up to my room. "At first I thought maybe that wasn't such a great career for a Christian. But then I really prayed about it, and you know what suddenly hit me?"

"What?"

"Well, if Christians don't get involved in the design world, then who's going be in control of what's going on in fashion?"

I nodded, then pulled the top that she'd taken in for me over my head. "Yeah, that's a good point. I know that I, for one, am getting a little sick and tired of lingerie companies constantly shoving their stupid push-up bras in my face."

"And the same thing goes with movies and music and, well, you name it. If we don't get involved in these things, then we have no right to complain about our limited options."

"Right on," I said as I pulled up the leather

skirt she'd insisted was perfect for me yesterday.

"That's why I'm changing my major next fall."

"Cool."

"Speaking of cool." Beanie stepped back and surveyed my outfit. "You look really hot."

I turned around and studied myself in the mirror. "It's kind of weird seeing my legs though. I usually wear long pants."

"Well, you have great legs, Chloe. Why not enjoy them?"

I laughed. "Actually I do. They work pretty well for me."

"I think you should wear tights with this outfit." She got a thoughtful look. "Maybe something in eggplant."

"Really?"

"Yeah, it'd look great next to the brown leather. And I think your Doc Martens are perfect. Keeps the urban thing going."

"Good. And I really like this top; it fits great now."

"Yeah, aren't those laces groovy?"

I nodded. "It's amazing. I don't know how you could figure all this out."

She grinned. "Maybe Caitlin's right. Maybe it is a gift."

"Oh yeah, it's definitely a gift." And I really believe that's true. The way Beanie helped the three of us pull outfits together—really cool

outfits—was nothing short of amazingly miracu-
lous. And each outfit suits our different personalities, and yet they all look good together too.
Even my mom seemed suitably impressed. Oh, sure,
it's not what she would've chosen, but I know she
felt it was an improvement.

"And who knows," I told Beanie as I carefully
set my new threads aside. "Maybe I'll start
dressing like this more often. It does feel more
creative."

She smiled. "Yeah, that's how clothes should
be—creative—an expression of who you really
are."

"But I plan to keep my hair like this, and I'm
not touching my piercings. And I don't really
think I can give up the urban thing, not completely."

Beanie agreed. "It's who you are," she said.
"It's not as if you need to go out and lose or even
alter your total identity. You just need to go
with your instincts and bring it to the surface
more."

Allie and Laura were as pleased as I was when
they came to practice today and picked up their
clothes.

"If we get a contract, we should hire Beanie as
our fashion consultant," said Laura.

"Yeah," agreed Allie in a deep businesslike
voice. "Sign her up. Put her on the payroll."

I laughed. "Yeah, then we'd better get to work here, make sure we do everything possible to get that contract."

"Watch out, Chloe's getting out her whip now." Allie got a sly look. "You know, when Beanie said she could see you in leather, I thought for sure she meant like black leather with big silver studs and probably a big whip just so you could beat us into shape."

Laura laughed.

But I felt slightly hurt. "You really think of me like that?"

Allie shrugged. "Just lately."

"It's okay," said Laura as she strapped on her bass. "Sometimes we need a hard taskmaster to keep us on track."

"And that's why I'm here," called Willy as he came up the stairs. "Aren't you girls even warmed up yet?"

"Just getting started." I began tuning my guitar.

Then, as if to prove that he could be a far worse taskmaster than me, Willy had us work all afternoon, plus we had to do a couple of songs over and over until all three of us were getting totally sick of them.

"Maybe we're just tired," I finally suggested.

"Yeah, we've been working really hard every single day," added Laura. "My fingers are sore."

"And I've got to be at the Paradiso in half an hour," said Allie.

"You girls quitting on me?" He looked slightly irked.

"Just for the night." I sighed and set down my guitar.

"And I was going to give you girls the day off tomorrow," he said.

"Well, it is Sunday." Laura reminded him.

He nodded with a look of realization. "Yeah, maybe I am getting a little too obsessed here. Sorry 'bout that, ladies. I just want to see you at your best."

I walked over and patted him on the back. "It's okay, Willy. We know it's only because you believe in us."

He brightened. "Yeah. And before I forget, you girls were looking pretty good earlier anyway—looking like you were really happy—"

"We were happy then." Allie picked up her pack. "But now we're tired."

"I know." He looked at his watch. "Guess I lost track of the time."

"Anyone wanna give me a ride to the Paradiso?" asked Allie.

"Sure." Laura snapped her bass case shut. "If you're ready to go right now. I've got to get home in time to change—I've got a date with Ryan at seven tonight."

Allie rolled her eyes at Laura. "Hey, don't rub it in." Then she turned to me. "Why don't you stop by the Paradiso tonight, Chloe? Cesar's probably going to be there."

Of course, I could hear Laura questioning Allie about Cesar as the two of them headed down the stairs before us. I wanted to strangle Allie.

"Got a boyfriend?" asked Willy.

I shook my head. "Only in Allie's imagination."

He grinned. "Well, I imagine you girls are going to have all kinds of boys wanting to be your boyfriends before too long. Success can really mess with your head, you know. You girls will have to learn to watch out for who's for real and who's not."

I laughed. "Hey, you're our manager, Willy. Aren't you supposed to deal with that when the time comes?"

"No problem. I'll just start packing my baseball bat whenever you girls are out in public."

"You'd really—?"

"No, I'm just pulling your leg."

But Willy did get me to thinking again. Not about my relationship with Cesar, because in all fairness, he's been my good friend long before our band became a reality—and besides, we're not really dating. Well, not yet anyway. But some other things happened tonight at the Paradiso that got me a little worried. It's as though I was watching something unfold that could become a problem. But I hope, I really hope, I'm wrong.

It was pretty busy when I arrived at the Paradiso, and so I decided to help out a little. I do this from time to time, and Mike always appreciates it, plus it kind of makes me feel more like I belong there. And I have to admit I was a little jealous when Allie started working there this week, and I was thinking, "Why didn't I take that job?" But on the other hand, I think it was right for me to stay focused on my music, and I'm sure I've written about six new songs just this week alone. Okay, they might not be good songs, but at least I took the time to actually write them down.

A lot of my songs begin really simply. Many of them start out as these poems, right here in this very diary. Hey, if I ever become famous this diary could become valuable. Or not. But so many of the songs just spring out of my life and how I feel about things. Then I take the lyrics to the next level, putting them to music. Some words just seem to want to sing—it's like they can't help themselves. I'm not sure how else to explain it. To me it's all very simple. I realize that most people think it must be so difficult, but for me it's almost as easy as breathing. I guess that's what makes this whole thing a gift.

But back to the Paradiso tonight. Anyway, I'm

making myself useful by taking the orders out to tables while Allie works the counter, and I notice Taylor Russell and a couple of his buddies waiting to place their orders. Nothing strange about that. But unless I'm imagining it, it looks as if Taylor is actually flirting with Allie.

To appreciate this, you need to understand that Allie is really in her element working at the Paradiso. It's like she totally fits in. And tonight she's wearing this new blouse that she found when we went shopping with Beanie. It's peach-colored and lacy and looks pretty spectacular with her beaded earrings. And I can tell that she's just eating up Taylor's attention. I'm sure he can tell too. And I'm making a mental note to tell Allie not to act so eager. It sends, I'm sure, the wrong message. But really, what do I know about such things?

Finally, the place settles down a little and I spot Cesar, Jake, and Marissa sitting down at a table by the window. I notice an empty chair and go over and ask to join them, still keeping an eye on Taylor and Allie.

"Sit down." Cesar smiles and actually pulls out the chair for me. He's such a gentleman.

"You mean you actually want to sit with the riffraff?" Marissa speaks in what seems a slightly aggravated tone. And I remember her ongoing crush on Cesar. Does she suspect some-

thing's going on between the two of us? Not that
there's anything to suspect.

"Real funny." I give her a look as I sit down,
then suddenly remember I forgot to order a cappuccino for myself.

"Do you work here too?" asks Jake.

"Nah, just helping out." I study him closely. I
know something's different about him but can't
quite put my finger on it. Finally I ask, "What'd
you do, Jake, change your hair or something?"

He sort of smiles, then rubs his lower lip. "My
rings...they're gone."

"Oh yeah. But why'd you do that?"

Cesar laughs. "They were freaking out my mom.
She thought Jake looked like a vampire. She was
calling him Vampiro Roho—the redheaded vampire."

"Did you mind taking them out?" I ask.

He shrugs. "Not really. It'll help me to get a
job too."

Just then Allie comes up and plops a big cappuccino in front of me. "On the house, from Mike."
Then she leans over and whispers, "Did you see
him?"

"Huh?" I look at her. "You mean Mike?"

She shakes her head then bends down again. "I
mean Taylor," she whispers.

I glance over to where Taylor and his buddies
are sitting then nod. "Yeah, I saw him."

"What's up, Al?" asks Cesar curiously.

Then she giggles—something she should <u>never</u> do in public. It makes her look like a total airhead. She shrugs. "Not much. Better get back to work."

"What's with <u>her</u>?" asks Marissa, still seeming to be irritated.

And suddenly I want to ask, "What's with you?" Instead I say, "I think Al's just getting excited about Nashville." Not entirely untrue.

"When do you guys leave anyway?" asks Jake.

"Monday." I sip my cappuccino and keep a discreet eye on Taylor. He is most definitely flirting with Allie. And she is flirting right back. And the whole thing makes me feel very uneasy.

"See, it's happening already," I hear Marissa saying.

"What's that?" I ask.

"You." She points at me. "Already you have your head in the clouds. It's like you're so caught up in this whole music thing that you don't even know we're here."

I look directly at her now. "That's not true. I was just thinking about something else."

"Yeah, like becoming a superstar snob."

I glance at Cesar, hoping for some moral support. And thankfully he comes through. "Chloe has a lot on her mind right now."

"Yeah," says Jake. "If she wanted to be a snob,

she wouldn't be sitting with us, would she?"

Marissa doesn't respond to this.

"You know, it's not easy for us either," I say as I glance over to Taylor, who's now standing very close to Allie, towering over her and looking at her like—well, like something not very nice. "And everyone's treating us differently. Like the people who used to ignore us have suddenly turned into our best buddies. And then there are others who we thought were real friends, and they're starting to act like they hate us now. It's pretty confusing, you know?"

"Yeah." Marissa rolls her eyes. "I feel so sorry for you."

"Lighten up, Marissa," says Jake in a sharp voice. "You're really becoming a drag."

Cesar nods. "Yeah, you should be happy for Chloe. She's worked really hard to get here, and she—"

"You're both doing such a bang-up job of being happy for her." Marissa stands abruptly. "I don't know why she needs my help."

"Marissa," I begin, hoping to smooth this over.

"Forget it!" She takes off.

"Man." Jake exhales. "That chick is just way too heavy for me."

"I think she's frustrated," I say, remembering something. "And I think I know how she feels."

"You feel like that?" asks Jake.

"Not right now. But I used to. It's like she's caught between two worlds and isn't sure which way to go—you know?"

Jake nods. "Oh, yeah. I guess I wasn't looking at it like that. I was just thinking this girl has a real attitude. Now, I feel kind of cruddy for razzing her." He glances out the window to where she's standing on the sidewalk smoking a cigarette like she's in some kind of a puffing marathon. "Maybe I should go talk to her."

Cesar shrugs. "Probably wouldn't hurt."

With that, Jake takes off, and now it's just Cesar and me.

"So, how are you doing really?" Cesar looks into my eyes as if he can detect something there.

"The truth is, I'm feeling a little worried for Al at the moment."

"For Al? Why?"

"It's probably dumb, but Taylor Russell is here tonight. And, well, Allie's had this stupid crush on him—"

"Like half the other girls in school."

"Yeah, but now I can tell that he's noticing her back. It's like he's coming on to her and..."

"And?"

"Oh, I'm not really sure. And I don't like to believe gossip. But something about this whole thing just bugs me."

He nods now. "I can understand that."

"You can? You don't think I'm being stupid?"

"No. I think you're being a good friend. Taylor definitely has a reputation with the girls."

"As in a use-'em-and-lose-'em reputation?"

He nods again. "Man, if you girls only knew half the stuff that's said in the locker room."

"I hate to even think about it. But Allie's not stupid. I'm sure she's heard about some of that stuff. I know I've suggested that Taylor's a jerk more than once." I glance at Cesar. "Do you think that's wrong? Am I being too judgmental?"

"Not when you know Taylor and his problem with ADD."

"You mean attention deficit disorder?"

"Yeah, but only when it comes to girls. He has the attention span of a termite when it comes to hanging in there with a relationship. Anyway, you probably won't have to worry about him for too long. Especially since you guys will be gone in a few days. By the time Allie gets back he'll probably have a new girl."

"Poor Allie."

"So, is that the only thing bugging you tonight, Chloe? You seem kind of down."

I shrug. "I guess that's mainly it. There's just so much going on right now. It's like I can hardly wrap my mind around everything all at once. It's pretty overwhelming."

"Yeah, I suppose I should back off too."

"Back off?"

He sets his cup down. "You know, give you some space. Not be one of those guys pushing into your world right before you become a superstar."

"If I hear that word one more time tonight, I might do something really scary."

He holds his hands up. "Okay, okay. But I think you know what I mean."

"I'm not sure I do. What exactly are you saying?"

He glances around now, as if to see if anyone is listening. "Chloe, you know I've liked you since the first day we met. And you're constantly doing this push-pull thing with me. Like you don't want to date, and that's okay, but then you want to be friends, and that's great, but then you start to act like maybe there could be something more, and..."

I feel my cheeks growing warm now. Had I really sent all those mixed-up signals? And even if I had, how perceptive is Cesar to actually catch and process them like that? And they say guys aren't sensitive. Well, I'm pretty impressed. I take a deep breath. "Okay, if I'm hearing you right, you're saying that you're confused."

"Yeah, that pretty much describes it."

"Well, so am I."

He smiles. "So we're at the same place then?"

"Maybe." I take in a deep breath and decide to

give this a shot. "Okay, the best relationship I can have with anyone is when I can be totally honest."

"Feel free."

"Okay, I really do like you, Cesar—"

"But—"

"No..." I look at him, noticing how nice he looks in his black T-shirt. "No buts. I really do like you. I'm just not sure what to do with it. And there's so much going on with the band and Nashville and—"

He brightened. "But you really do like me?"

I look into his eyes now and suddenly feel as if I'm getting lost in there—those deep brown pools—it's like I'm fighting to catch my breath. "Cesar," I say, trying to calm myself. "I honestly don't know what's going to happen next. I don't know what to—"

"But you really do like me?" He persists with this sweet crooked smile.

"Yes. I really do like you—a lot. And I guess it actually scares me a little."

He reaches over now and, to my surprise, takes my hand. It's such a tender gesture, and I feel this warm rush go through me—it's almost electrical, and good, but slightly frightening. "I really do like you too, Chloe. And I'm willing to leave it at that for now. Honestly, I don't want to pressure you. I know you have a lot on your plate right now. I just want to be here for you."

My eyes grow wide. "You do?"

"Yeah. That's enough for me for the time being."

"Cool." Now I'm thinking, "I think I love this guy!" Okay, slow down, Chloe girl. Take a deep breath. Just breathe and chill.

"Yeah," he continues, "And if I do anything that puts pressure on you, I want you to tell me to knock it off. Okay?"

"Okay."

"I mean it."

And so, with that out of the way, we just sit there and gab. He tells me about his parents. How his dad worked his way up to a management position at an accounting firm and how his mom works part-time in a florist shop. He explains how his little sister Abril despises middle school and thinks everyone there is childish and immature. I tell him about how much I hated my last year of middle school and how my so-called friends betrayed me. Then I go on to tell him a little more about my family, even about Caleb. I don't usually talk about him—not to anyone.

"When was the last time you saw him?"

"Wow, let's see...I'd say it's been at least three years. I remember it was really a bad scene. My parents were fed up and told him not to come around anymore until he cleaned up his act. They called it tough love at the time. But it seemed pretty harsh to me."

"Maybe, but don't kid yourself. Drugs are pretty harsh too. I've seen too many people totally mess up their lives with drugs. I don't think there's any real easy answers there."

"Yeah, but I just wish I could tell Caleb that I love him."

"Maybe you'll get the chance."

We talk on and on about dozens of things. And it's strange because it seems we could go on like this forever—fortunately for me, since I decided early on to stay until closing, or until Taylor leaves, whichever comes first, to make sure Allie doesn't do something stupid. Finally, Mike is hinting that it's time to call it a night. But Taylor's still here. Cesar knows about my plan, and he gets up and says good night, then I go over to the counter where Allie is wiping down the big copper machine.

"Need a ride home, Al?"

She tosses me a look as if to clue me in that something's up, then she nonchalantly says, "Not tonight, Chloe. Taylor offered to take me home." Just like that happens all the time.

Okay, I'll admit I'm being overly protective of her. Why is that? Even though she's younger than me and on the petite side, she's not a child. And yet she seems so innocent and vulnerable sometimes. I

can't really explain it. "Are you sure?" I ask,
sending her, I hope, a message that says this
might not be such a good idea.

But she just laughs. "Of course. He's right
there waiting."

I look over and he nods at me. And I'm thinking he's thinking, "Just beat it, chick." And so I
do. But even now I feel bad.

KEEP US SAFE
watch over Your lambs
big and small
keep us safe
one and all
keep the hungry
wolves at bay
watch Your lambs
by night and day
care and give us
what we need
Living Water
grass to feed
watch over Your lambs
keep Your sheep
ever safe
while we sleep
amen

Sixteen

Monday, June 16

I can't believe it; it's finally happening. We're on our way to Nashville—first class too! Willy and my dad are sitting together and Laura's with her mom. Meanwhile, Allie and I are sitting by ourselves in front. We're wearing these wire-rimmed sunglasses and pretending we've already made it to the big times, acting as if we're trying not to be recognized by our admiring fans. Kind of dumb, but fun. Besides, this might be as good as it gets—our return trip might be all gloomy and sad if we don't get offered a contract. So we're thinking, hey, we may as well enjoy what we have right now. Ah, the beauty of living one day at a time!

"Taylor called me this morning to say good-bye," Allie informs me shortly after we board the plane.

"Really?"

She nods, suppressing, I can tell, great excitement. "Every single day since Saturday, we've either done something together or he's called me on the phone."

"Uh-huh." I flip through my magazine and hope to appear uninterested.

"Is that all you can say? Uh-huh? Sheesh, I wish I was sitting with Laura now."

"Okay, so what do you think is happening between you guys?"

She smiles in a dreamy way. "I think he's got it bad for me."

"Uh-huh." I'm glad she can't see me rolling my eyes beneath these shades.

"There you go—"

"Sorry. So, he's got it bad for you. How do you feel about him?"

She leans back into the comfy leather seat and sighs. "Pretty good."

Now I'm thinking...what to do here? Tell her what Cesar said about the locker room, that I think Taylor is a major jerk? What?

"Taylor says that I'm not like any other girl he's ever known."

"That's nice."

"Nice?" She turns and even from behind her sunglasses I can feel the glare. "Is that the best you can do, Chloe?"

"I don't know, Al. I'm not sure what I think about Taylor."

"Oh, don't start getting all judgmental on me now."

"I'm not being judgmental."

"Then what is it? Do you really <u>know</u> Taylor? I mean, it's obvious he doesn't look like the kind of guy you'd be interested in, but that doesn't mean there's something wrong with him. Besides, you're the one always going on about not judging by appearances."

"It's not his appearance..." But then I'm wondering if that isn't partly true because Taylor does have those movie-star good looks. Tall, muscular, tan, with sandy brown hair and white teeth. In some ways, he reminds me a little of Josh. But that's no reason to dislike him.

"Well, what is it then?"

"You know he sort of has a reputation—"

"I knew it!" She snaps her fingers in my face. "You're judging him only because of gossip you've heard. Well, how fair is that? I mean, how do you like it when people go around doing that about you? Like how about that time everyone said you beat Kerry up and broke her nose? How'd that make you feel?"

"But it wasn't true."

"And you know for a fact that what you've heard about Taylor is true?"

I shake my head. I consider telling her what Cesar said, but I hate draggin' him into this. "No, it's just a strong feeling I have."

Allie leans back now and folds her arms across her chest. "Well, it's not fair, Chloe. You should get to know him personally before you write him off like that. I expected more from you."

I consider what Cesar said about Taylor's attention span and imagine him hooking up with some other girl while we're gone. "Yeah, you're probably right, Al. I don't really know him."

"So, you're willing to give him a chance?"

I shrug. "Like it matters."

She leans forward and tips up her glasses now and looks me right in the eyes. "It does matter. It matters to me. I want you to like my boyfriend."

Boyfriend? But having some wits about me, I keep my mouth shut and turn the page on the magazine.

"Speaking of guys..." I hear the lilting tone of her voice and I know exactly where she's going. "You and Cesar seemed pretty cozy on Saturday night. What's going on with you guys these days?"

And so, relieved to change the subject from Taylor, I tell her a little bit about our conversation and how we're open to what lies ahead, but in no hurry to rush things.

"Cesar is so cool." She smiles. "And he's deep too. He really thinks about things. I like that."

Now I'm feeling all guilty like I should say something positive about Taylor. But what? I refuse to be a phony. "You know who Taylor reminds me of just a little?" I finally say in desperation.

"Brad Pitt?"

I laugh. "No. In some ways, he reminds me of Josh."

This seems to please her. "Well, then you should like him."

I nod, but I'm thinking, "I didn't really like Josh when he was in high school."

And so I'm sitting here writing all this down, all the while wondering about what's going to happen in Nashville. We'll arrive this afternoon and have a free day tomorrow. Then the big day is on Wednesday. It's way too early to be this nervous.

BEGINNING AGAIN

give me peace

calm my soul

soothe my spirit

make me whole

make me new

a fresh start

cleanse me, Lord

fill my heart

cm

Tuesday, June 17

Today was a good day for distractions. We toured the Grand Ole Opry, the old historic building that is, which is really much smaller than you'd think. It reminded me of a church with its wooden benches and stained glass windows. And even

though I'm not a country music fan, it was easy to
feel awed to think of all those long-gone per-
formers who once stood on that stage. People like
Patsy Cline. I must admit to watching the movie
about her life once, when it was on that women's
channel, and I thought she was, after all, pretty
cool. And what a voice! Of course, I never admitted this to anyone else before.

So the day has finally come to an end, and
we're back at the hotel now—which is pretty nice.
It's actually an old train station that's been
remodeled into this really cool hotel. The lobby
is enormous with lots of marble and skylights
and statues. You can just feel the history here.
And everything in our rooms feels very elegant—
even the soaps are French—and we girls have
been enjoying our pretense of being rich and
famous. Of course, this might all come to an
abrupt end tomorrow. But for now it's fun.

We've tried not to talk about tomorrow's audition; it only seems to make us more nervous. And
like Willy says, "What will be will be." But it
does seem weird that we haven't practiced in two
whole days. I'm trying not to worry about how this
will affect our performance tomorrow. It's not as
if we ever used to practice every day before, but
last week was kind of like cramming, and now it
feels as though we're slacking just a bit.

We just finished watching, of all things, this

goofy movie about a band that records one song and really makes it big. It was pretty funny, but at the same time a little depressing because the band ends up breaking up just when they start becoming really successful. I hope that's not what happens to us. Although the mere thought of even making one song that's a hit seems almost worth the breaking up part—but not really. Because I really do love Allie and Laura and don't like the idea of losing our friendship at all. Anyway, we three agreed that we'll keep our friendship above our music. More important, we will keep God as our number one priority.

I'm sure everyone else is asleep by now, but I'm too excited to sleep. And this worries me because I don't want to be all worn out and frazzled when we audition tomorrow. And so I will sign off and pray for slumber.

ALL YOURS
my hopes
my dreams
my highest aspirations
are in Your hands
o God
my life
my love
all that i am
is in Your hands

my God
hold me
keep me
protect me
i am Yours
amen

Wednesday, June 18

The big day is now over. Tah-dah!

We toured the recording company and met so many people that I'll never possibly remember all those names. Not that I'll need to. I'm sure that I don't need to, since I'll probably never see any of them again. Okay, I don't know this for certain. We know nothing for certain. All we know is that, "We'll be getting hold of you." That's what Eric Green said as he shook each of our hands after the audition.

The audition. Hmmm. I guess it went okay. Not perfectly. Not nearly as well as the memorial concert last month. But we did the best we could under the circumstances. It's hard to be comfortable when it feels as though you're under a gigantic magnifying glass. It didn't help that I had a big zit trying to pop out in the center of my chin. You know the kind that are red and hard and feel like Mount St. Helens just before it erupts and wreaks havoc everywhere. Allie insisted on putting a little cover-up on it and promised that it was invisible, although it felt very visible to me. But I won't go on about that.

They gave us about an hour to warm up and get everything set with the sound technicians. And we were actually starting to relax a little, and I thought maybe this won't be so bad after all. Willy was really hanging loose, cracking jokes, and basically keeping us light and on track—or trying to.

But then it was ten o'clock and here came six men and one woman, all in very expensive-looking dark suits. They all seemed to be about the age of our parents or older. Two of the men looked like they were close to sixty. And okay, I just don't get that. Why were these old suit people making decisions about who did or did not get a recording contract? I mean, they're not the kind of people who would ever go out and buy our kind of music in the first place, so why should they get to be the judge of whether it's good or not?

It's not as if I expected to see a bunch of kids our age walking in and offering us a record deal, but I guess I expected people who looked just a little more music-minded or even trendy. Now in Eric's defense, he seemed more like a music guy. And he didn't even have on a suit, just nice pants and a dark shirt. But here I go again, judging the book by its cover, and this is something I totally dislike for people to do to me. Am I becoming shallow???

Maybe so. Because as soon as we met the suits, I started to feel a little uncomfortable with my "peculiar" hair color and piercings and stuff. I felt like I was standing in front of my mom—times seven! As if I was being scrutinized for every detail that did not, would never, measure up to what I'm sure they thought a decent Christian girl should be.

I was thinking, "Did I forget that this is a Christian recording company?" Who knows what they might've expected? Suddenly, just as we're about to begin, I imagined that the last group in here was dressed in matching light blue suits and singing Southern gospel music in four-part harmony, and I thought, "What in the world are we doing here?"

Just the same, we played. And although we were understandably nervous, there was no barfing on guitars or stage fright or missed notes or false starts. In fact, we did okay. Willy said we played beautifully, but then he was probably just being nice.

The seven suits were all very polite and told us that we were good and certainly must have a bright future ahead of us, but their smiles were tight, and their handshakes stiff, and it felt as if they were covering something up. Like they were thinking, "Eric Green, you are fired! How dare you bring this sorry excuse for a band in here! What were you thinking?" About that time, Eric delivered his line about him being in touch. I almost expected him to say, "Don't call us, we'll call you." Or, "Here's your hat what's your hurry?"

My dad and Laura's mom both assured us that Willy was right and that we sounded great. "You did your best," Dad said, putting his arm around my shoulders as we walked out to the two cabs already waiting for us. "You've got nothing to feel ashamed about."

But as we packed our things into the trunk, I felt absolutely miserable. It was all I could do to keep from crying. I felt like this was our one big chance, and we simply weren't good enough. We hadn't made the grade.

I still don't know how Allie and Laura feel about the whole thing. We girls rode together, and we were all pretty quiet on the ride back to the hotel. I'm sure everyone's just tired. I know I was. And suddenly I wish we were going home today—I'd like to go hide in my room and have a good cry—but our flight home isn't until tomorrow.

Back at the hotel, Willy and Dad invited us to go sightseeing again today, but we three girls declined. And Mrs. Mitchell looked relieved. I had a feeling she was ready to go home too.

"Guess you ladies are all worn out," said Willy.

And maybe that's it. I know I, for one, am ready for a nice long nap. Maybe when I wake up I'll realize that today was just a dream. That we haven't done the audition yet, and we have another chance, and that somehow we'll get it right this time. We'll really wow them. Or maybe not.

THE BREAKS
i guess i'll live
it'll be okay
life goes on
just another day
back to normal
is where i'll go
and i'll be fine
take it slow
it's just how
cookies crumble
that's the breaks
take a tumble
que sera and
carry on
trust in God
sing a song
cm

Seventeen

Thursday, June 19

Well, morning comes and I'm ready to blow this joint. Okay, it's really a nice hotel, but I'm thinking, "Get me outta here! I wanna go home!" And then the phone rings. I hear my dad pick it up, and I stop shoving stuff into my backpack and just freeze, straining to listen.

"Is that so?" I hear him say. "Maybe you should talk to Chloe." Then he's calling out to me to get the phone.

I pick up the receiver in my adjoining room and say, "Hello?"

"Hey, Chloe, this is Eric. Whazzup?"

"Not much." It bugs me when grown-ups say "whazzup."

He kind of chuckles then. "Well, I just thought you might like to know that we want to offer Redemption a contract."

Just then my knees turn to Jell-O, and I'm not sure if I can speak coherently.

"Chloe? You still there?"

"Uh—yeah. Did I hear you—?"

"You heard me right." He laughs. "This is always the best part of my job. I love hearing the reactions."

"But did you actually say—?"

"I'm saying that we want to offer you girls a recording contract. I've asked your dad to postpone your return flight until tomorrow so we can bring you back over to Omega this afternoon and go over some things."

"You're kidding?" I think I'm actually screaming now, and I hope I haven't permanently damaged his hearing.

He laughs again. "Nope, it's really true. Now I'm going to call Willy and start hammering out some of the preliminary details. I'm guessing you might want to go tell the rest of your band."

"Yeah, of course, you bet. Thanks! Thanks so much. This is so—" Now I'm actually starting to cry. "This is so cool!"

"I couldn't agree more. And I honestly think Redemption is going to be a really big hit."

Then I hang up and start walking around my room in crooked little circles, muttering, I think, something that probably sounds unintelligible, but really I'm sure I'm thanking God.

"You going to tell the others?" Dad is standing in the doorway watching me with an amused expression.

I run over and hug him, tears streaming down

my face. "Can you believe it, Dad? Can you believe it?"

He laughs and nods. "Yeah, I think I almost can."

"I've got to tell Allie and Laura," I scream, close to hysteria again. It's all just so unbeliev-able. Somehow I make it to their adjoining rooms, and the next thing I know we're all three in the hallway, jumping and yelling and totally going nuts while the three adults stand around and smile. Well, except for Laura's mom. She's not really smiling. Actually she looks just slightly bewildered.

"It's like a dream," says Allie with tears in her eyes.

"Somebody pinch me," says Laura.

So I do.

"Youch!" But she laughs.

"I've gotta call my mom." Allie suddenly bolts for her room.

"I've got to call Dad," says Laura to her mom.

"We better call your mom too," Dad reminds me with a wink. "She might want to start looking for the right lawyer to go over the contract."

Willy waves his hand. "Don't worry. We won't have to sign anything today. We'll just meet with the folks at Omega and go over a few things. Then we'll take copies of the contract home to read more carefully at our leisure. Since the kids are

all minors, they need to have their parents sign.
And it might not hurt to have a lawyer go over
everything."

And then everyone disperses to use the phones
and change flights and schedule appointments,
etc., etc. When Dad gets off the phone I must
remember to call Mike at the Paradiso like I
promised. Will he really call the newspaper?
Maybe I should tell him to hold off until we know
more about what exactly is being offered to us.
Although the mere idea that Omega is offering
anything at all is enough for me.

Anyway, I'm back in my hotel room just feeling
totally stunned and overwhelmed as I write all
this down. It's so unreal. I mean, we've dreamed of
this day, and we even believed it could happen.
But now it feels just like Allie said, like it's all
a wonderful dream and someone's going to come in
here and wake me up and tell me it's time to go to
school or mow the lawn or something.

BIG THANKS!
thank You, God
even if it's a dream
it's a good one
thank, You, God
for doing something
so incredibly huge
and amazing

and wonderful
<u>only You</u>
could do this
thank You, God
amen

Friday, June 20

We're flying home now—first class again—and this time we're no longer <u>pretending</u> to be celebrities. Okay, maybe it is a little premature to start thinking we're all rich and famous (heh-heh), but it is more than just a fantasy now. And slowly, it's starting to feel less like a dream and more like reality.

After our celebration dinner yesterday, we three girls made a pact. Eric and a couple of the other "suits" (who were really quite nice despite their somewhat intimidating appearances) took us to this really fancy restaurant. And anyway, we three girls made a pact in the rest room—of all places—and we promised that no matter how famous we might become (and who knows, we might), we will <u>never</u> let the success go to our heads, we will <u>never</u> become demanding divas, we will <u>never</u> forget our old friends, and we'll <u>always</u> keep our friendship <u>above</u> the music.

And I'm writing all this down today just in case any of us ever forgets! Not that I think we will, but you never know. I remember what happened in the movie "That Thing You Do!" and how everyone started turning against each other. But really, I don't think that could happen to us. We have God to keep us glued together, and we love each other like sisters!

But anyway, here's what happened when we went back to Omega. We were ushered (all six of us) into the president's conference room, where we all sat in sleek black leather chairs around a dark wooden table that was as shiny as glass. I could actually see my reflection in the surface.

Mr. Sallinger, the president of Omega (the oldest of the "suits," with gray hair) was at the head of the table. And Eric was sitting to his right. "We're so pleased here at Omega to have the opportunity to record your music. We were all very impressed with Redemption yesterday, and we think you girls have what it takes to go the distance." He studied our faces. "To be honest, we've never recorded a girl band before, but as you can see—" he waved his arm to the numerous photos displayed on his office walls, one band in particular that I recognized because they've been extremely popular in both Christian and regular circles—"we've recorded some of the best musicians in the industry." He smiled broadly. "So you'll be in good company. And we think you'll fit in just fine. Eric has the contracts all printed up for you. It's our boiler-plate contract—"

"That means it's basically the same contract that we offer to all our first-time recording musicians," Eric quickly explained.

"That's right." Mr. Sallinger smiled at Eric. "And naturally, if you have any questions or concerns, we're more than happy to answer them. Eric's your man for that."

Now Eric was handing each of us a thick yellow legal-sized envelope. "We can go over some of the preliminaries while you're all here, if you like."

Mr. Sallinger stood. "Now, if you'll all excuse me, I have an important meeting already scheduled, but I just wanted to take some time to welcome Redemption into the Omega family." He nodded with what seemed genuine satisfaction. "We're so very pleased to have you joining our recording family. And it's plain to see that God has blessed you girls with some outstanding talent. Now, I'll leave Eric to field your questions."

Then we all opened our envelopes and I just sort of blinked at the stack of typed pages—single-spaced and filled with lots of words I don't even know. And I usually think of myself as having a fairly decent vocabulary.

"This looks like Greek to me," said Allie with a goofy grin.

Eric laughed. "Hey, you're not alone there. The truth is most people can't make heads or tails of recording contracts. Let me just take you over the highlights."

And the highlights were (if I can remember) that we sign with Omega for one year, with an agreement to two more years (if things go well), and we three girls will equally split what sounded like pretty huge sum to me (even if it wasn't the "million" that Allie was hoping for), but which Willy told Eric "is yet to be determined." And I was thinking, "Watch it, Willy, we don't want to blow this deal before we even get signed up." But, thankfully, I kept my mouth closed. After all, he _is_ our manager. And last but not least, we must be willing to tour for six months of the year.

"_Six_ months?" exclaimed Laura's mother as if we were being assigned hard labor or a prison sentence.

Eric nodded. "Yes, that's standard. To _sell_ albums we must _promote_ albums. The girls have to create a name for themselves. The only way to do that is to tour and perform live."

"Six months?" she said again. "But what about school?"

"Tutors." Eric looked at her evenly, and I could tell he was wondering if she was going to be the wrench in the works. I know I was getting worried.

"I'd like to be tutored," I said brightly.

"Me too," echoed Allie.

Laura remained silent, just watching her mother.

"But the girls are so young," she continued. "Why, Laura's the oldest and she's only sixteen and a half. And as her mother I'm not entirely sure I want her traveling all over God's creation, doing who knows what with who knows whom, on some broken-down bus that—"

Eric loudly cleared his throat. "We provide a top-of-the-line motor coach with everything these girls could possibly need—including full bathroom, TV, VCR, full kitchen, microwave. It even has a washer and dryer. We cover all expenses including the cost of one adult chaperone."

"Sounds great to me." I smiled at Eric, not wanting anything to spoil this deal. Frankly, I was thinking the whole touring business sounded like a really exciting vacation.

"Well, I don't know." She shook her head.

"Mom," began Laura slowly. "I'm not a baby anymore. And I really want this."

Her mother gave her a sharp look, then quietly said, "We'll talk about this more when we get home."

Eric continued to go over a few more things, and I'm afraid I wasn't paying close attention just then because I was too busy imagining us on tour, performing in exciting places and staying in our luxury tour RV. Finally, Eric asked if we had any more questions.

"I think my wife wants to have an attorney go over the details," my dad explained. "How soon would you like to hear back from us?"

"I can understand wanting to have a lawyer look into this. That's fairly normal. But just the same, we don't like these things to drag out. Would two weeks be fair?"

I was thinking two days sounded more than fair to me, but once again, I kept my mouth shut.

"Two weeks should be just fine." Dad slipped his copy of the contract back into the envelope.

Eric turned to Willy now. "How about you, anything else you'd like to know?"

"Nope. I think you answered most of my questions over the phone when we spoke this morning. I'll go over this more carefully on our flight home tomorrow."

Eric stood and shook hands with everyone. "We are really excited about Redemption." He grinned. "We don't even want to change your name."

"Do you usually change names?" I asked.

He pointed to the picture of the band I had recognized. "Do you girls know who these guys are?"

"Of course," said Laura. "That's Iron Cross. Everyone knows them."

"Do you know what their original name was?"
None of us knew.

"The Baxter Boys."

"The Baxter Boys?" I laughed. "That sounds like something right out of the fifties."

Eric grinned. "Well, you probably know that two of these guys are brothers, Jeremy and Isaiah Baxter. But when they started doing music they were just little kids, and that's what everyone in the neighborhood called them. It was okay for church socials and playing around town, but a little hokey as they got older and more sophisticated."

I nodded. "Yeah, they do _not_ look like the Baxter Boys."

"Will we ever get to meet them?" asked Allie with that dreamy look again.

"As a matter of fact, we've been talking about the possibility of a joint tour. You girls could possibly open for them."

"We're going to open for Iron Cross?" I hoped I wasn't acting too starstruck, although I couldn't really help myself. Just the same, I did remind myself of Allie.

He nodded. "If everything goes as planned, I'd say it's a distinct possibility that Iron Cross and Redemption will be appearing together."

"Cool." Allie was still staring at the photo.

Laura just shook her head in amazement. And

I could tell that despite her mother's less-than-enthusiastic response, Laura wanted this as badly as Allie and I did. And then we left. But instead of cramming into a taxi like we'd done to get there, we found a big stretch limo waiting to take us back to the hotel. Talk about cool! It had leather everywhere, two TVs, and a minibar (complete with sodas, juice, and water), and we honestly felt as though we'd really made the big time.

And I guess, all things considered, we didn't make complete fools of ourselves the other day. I'm still a little concerned about Laura's mom's reaction. I'd hate to think that she's going to be the spoiler here. I'm sure Omega would NOT be interested in signing me and Allie and Willy. And even though Willy plays a pretty mean bass, somehow it just doesn't look quite right to have two teenage girls and this old dude.

YOUR WILL
what do You want, God?
i know what i want
i want to make music for You
but what about You?
what's Your will?
if this is Your will
i believe You'll work out
all the details

i'm trusting You for that
that's all i can do
is trust You
and wait
for Your will
amen

Eighteen

Monday, June 23

What a whirlwind ride these past few days have been. When we arrived at the airport (late Friday night), we were met by reporters as well as family and friends. It seemed that Mike had told everyone at the Paradiso about our pending contract. But I must admit that it was pretty cool being greeted by reporters and photographers (even if they were only from the local paper), and it was fun seeing balloons and signs of congratulations. And Cesar even brought me flowers (as did Ryan and Taylor for Laura and Allie). I was a little disappointed to see Taylor there (so much for Cesar's attention span theory). But I tried not to let that get to me, and I must admit Allie looked totally thrilled to see him.

Sunday, at church, was a little more of the same. The youth group had a big sign and Krispy Kreme donuts to celebrate. And after that I went home and had a late lunch with my parents and Josh, and then pretty much crashed, catching up on lost sleep since it seems I hardly slept at all in Nashville.

I woke up to Allie knocking on my door. "What

are you doing sleeping?" she demanded when she walked in.

I sat up and yawned. "Why not?"

"How can you possibly sleep when life is so totally exciting?"

I shrugged. "You gotta sleep sometime. What's up?"

"I just got done at the Paradiso, and Mike reminded me that we promised we'd perform this week, so I kind of agreed that we'd do it Tuesday night. Does that work for you?"

"Yeah, I don't think I'm booked that night."

"Well, I don't know about you, but I'm thinking we could use a little practice session."

"Uh-huh."

"So I called Laura and she's working all day tomorrow, so I told her why not this evening."

So we practiced all evening. Well, we mostly practiced. It seemed we spent more time than usual just gabbing about everything that's been happening and what's going to happen next.

It's been decided (by Willy) that we'll have a "business meeting" on Thursday evening. All parents will attend, and it'll be a time to ask questions and voice concerns. Willy will take notes, and my mom will tell everyone about the lawyer's initial reaction. And I guess we'll just take it from there.

"It doesn't seem fair," said Allie.

"What?" I asked as I tuned my guitar.

"That the grown-ups have all the power."

"All the power?" I peered over at her.

"Yeah, to make the decisions and sign the contract. But then we have to do all the work."

"Yeah," Laura agreed. "We should have an equal say."

"I thought we did."

"Not according to my mom," said Laura.

I considered this. Maybe they were right. "Well, I guess Thursday night is a good time for us to let them know what we think."

Laura nodded. "But we'll have to be tactful. If we start acting rude and uppity my mom will turn against us like that." She snapped her fingers. "If you haven't noticed, my mom is from the 'old school' where kids are supposed to be polite and respectful at all times."

"Yeah, I kind of noticed," I admitted.

So we decided to present our case, but not in a way that would get any of the grown-ups mad. We decided our best defense would be to act very mature, like we're old enough to handle these kinds of decisions and responsibilities. And I think we are.

Wednesday, June 25

We had a blast playing at the Paradiso last night. And it was packed out. But there was this

one weird moment, just as we finished a song,
when I suddenly remembered how totally freaked
I'd been last fall—the first time I'd ever played
in public—and how I'm so completely comfortable
with everything now. Somehow it just struck me
as slightly amazing.

We only played for an hour, then pretty much
enjoyed ourselves with everyone who was there.
And it seemed everyone was there. And everyone
came up and congratulated us and acted as if
they'd always been our very best friends.
Including Tiffany Knight. And it was a little
irritating too because it's like she wouldn't back
off. She just kept hanging on as though we were
best buddies. And I just don't get that. Has she no
pride at all? There's no way I could act like that
to someone I'd treated so poorly. I kept reminding
myself of how people treated Jesus, and how He
still loved and forgave them—and how we're supposed to do the same. So maybe Tiffany Knight is
my "cross to bear." It figures.

Caitlin and some of her college friends were
there too. Naturally Josh was sitting with them.
I went over to join them for a while, and even told
Beanie about what we'd said about having her as
our wardrobe consultant.

"Seriously?" she said.

"Yeah, if you'd like to. I guess we'll have to
make sure it's okay as far as our contract goes,

but I don't remember them saying anything about our clothes, and even if they did, we could tell them we want you involved."

"That'd be so cool."

Josh grinned. "I still can't believe my baby sister is almost famous."

Caitlin playfully punched him in the arm. "She IS famous, Josh. Didn't you see the Sunday paper? Sheesh, they were all over the front page."

I laughed. "Yeah, the distribution of that paper must be at least five thousand."

"Hey, it's a start," said Jenny. "We told Danny, you know, that drummer friend of mine from college, about what's going on with your band, and he was having a hard time not getting seriously jealous. I told him he should come hear you girls before he starts feeling too slighted." She laughed. "The truth is, Redemption is way better than his band. But I won't tell him that."

I was standing as I talked to them, and then Cesar came up from behind and put his arm around me. I'd already told him I'd hang with him tonight after we got done playing. But somehow, maybe it was the look on Caitlin's face, but suddenly I felt a little self-conscious.

"Uh, this is Cesar," I told everyone. Then I told him their names, and he politely reached out and shook hands.

"I remember you," he said to Caitlin. "You went

to visit Jewel in the hospital last year. She was
my cousin."

Caitlin's eyes grew thoughtful. "That was a
hard time."

He nodded then turned to Josh. "And I've heard
a lot about you."

Josh grinned. "That's scary."

We all visited a little longer, and I began to
relax more. But still I wanted to know what
Caitlin was thinking. Or maybe I didn't.

Finally, Cesar and I excused ourselves and
went over to join Laura and Ryan.

"Where's Al?" I asked, looking around the
crowded room.

"She left with Taylor." Laura peeked at her
watch. "Actually, I should probably get going too.
I have to work in the morning."

Cesar laughed. "I'd think you'd be quitting
that job, what with your newfound fame and fortune."

Laura shook her head. "Well, as far as fortune
goes, we haven't seen an actual penny yet."

"Yeah." I sighed. "And if we don't get those
contracts signed, we never will either."

"In the meantime I promised my parents I'd
stick to my job." Laura glanced at Ryan. "And keep
my curfews."

Ryan stood now. "Well, we better not disap-
point them."

And once again, it was just Cesar and me.

"Speaking of jobs," I asked him, "how's yours doing?"

He smiled. "I just got a raise."

"Cool."

"And they're putting me on full-time for the rest of the summer." Then he frowned. "Of course, that means I won't get to see as much of you."

"I'm sure we'll be able to squeeze some time in together."

He seemed relieved to hear me say this. "Yeah. And mostly I'm working days, except for Thursdays and Fridays when I get the late shift."

"That's not too bad. How's Jake doing? I haven't seen him around tonight. Or Marissa. What's up with her?"

"Yeah, I forgot to tell you about Jake. He got hired at Home Depot too. But since he's new, he got stuck with all evenings."

"Poor Jake."

"It might be a good thing. Doesn't give him any time to be tempted to go partying. Spencer is always trying to get him to go out with him, but so far, Jake's done pretty well."

"Is he still staying with you?"

He nodded. "But my parents say he's got to find someplace else in a few weeks."

"And he probably doesn't want to go home."

"Not at all. He and his dad aren't even speaking.

He's pretty sure his stepmom has told his dad all kinds of lies."

"Poor Jake."

"But he left a message with his uncle, his mom's brother, out in California. I guess he's on vacation now, but he was really close to Jake's mom, and he told Jake, after she died, to call if he ever needed anything."

"I'm going to be praying for Jake more than ever now."

"And I haven't seen Marissa since last week. But Jake said she got a job at Burger King."

I tried to imagine Marissa in one of those colorful outfits but couldn't. "I hope she's okay."

We talked some more, but then Cesar admitted that he too had to be to work early in the morning. "Can I give you a ride home?"

"Sure. Just let me go tell Josh that I'm going with you." So I went back over to the "college" table and informed Josh.

"So is this serious?" Caitlin asked me in a lowered voice. "Between you and Cesar, I mean?"

I shrugged. "I'm not sure what you mean by serious."

"Are you guys going out?" she asked.

"Sort of. We like each other, if that's what you mean."

She studied me for a moment then smiled. Okay, maybe it was a forced smile, I'm not sure. Then she said, "Well, he seems like a pretty nice guy."

I nodded. "He really is."

Cesar drove an old pickup that he's slowly restoring. I think it's very cool. "You're doing all this yourself?" I asked him as I admired the new paint job beneath the streetlights. It's a pale yellow, kind of like butter.

"Yeah. It's still got a long ways to go, but it's kind of fun. My dad's really into it too—it's something we can do together. And it helps getting my employee discount for tools and stuff."

"I keep telling my parents I need a car too," I said as we pulled up to my house. "But they keep brushing me off and telling me I can use theirs when I need to. Except that almost every time I need to they're gone, along with their cars, or at least their keys."

"Well, I don't mind giving you rides." He turned off his engine.

"Thanks."

"And I'm sure it's just a matter of time before you'll be able to afford any kind of car you'd like." There seemed to be a trace of sadness in his voice.

"Does that bother you?"

He shrugged. "Yeah, I guess so. It's kind of humiliating to think that my girlfriend is going to be way richer than me."

I laughed. But part of it was pure nervousness. It was the very first time I'd heard him refer to me as his "girlfriend." But at the same time, I did like the sound of it. "If you know me as well as you think you do, you should know that money isn't that important to me."

He laughed then. "Yeah, I suppose you'd do the whole music thing whether they paid you or not."

"You know, I probably would."

Then he reached over and ran his hand through my hair. "That's one of the many things I really love about you, Chloe."

Okay, the electricity was flowing then, and I was just sitting there and staring at him like a dummy. His face looked all shadowy and handsome in the dimly lit truck. And all I could think of was how I wanted him to kiss me. And how I wanted to kiss him back. Now was that so wrong? Really?

But instead of pulling me to him and passionately kissing me, he continued to talk. "I really believe that God brought you into my life for a purpose. Right from the beginning I could tell there was something special about you. And everything that's happened this year...well, it's just so amazing." He laughed. "In fact, my mom is dying to meet you."

"You're kidding."

"No, Jake's been telling her all about you, and she finally figured out that you're the girl I've been interested in all this time. She thinks

you're the one who got me to 'go back to church,' so
naturally she thinks you're wonderful. I haven't
really tried to explain that it had more to do with
me and God. But anyway, she'd love to meet you
sometime. So would Abril. After that article in
the paper, which Jake made certain my family saw,
they all think you're a celebrity."

"That's so funny."

"What's funny?"

"Oh, you know, that celebrity stuff. It still
just cracks me up."

His face grew serious then. "Well, you better
start getting used to it. Your life is going to be
changing pretty fast from now on."

I nodded. "It's kind of scary. But at the same
time exciting."

"Well, if anyone deserves it, Chloe, it's you."

"Thanks." I looked into his eyes then, and I
was thinking, "Come on, Cesar, just kiss me." But
still he didn't.

Instead, he took my hand in his and said, "You
know, I really don't want to blow this with you.
I've really been praying and asking God to show
me the right way to handle everything. But I'm
just not sure. I know I don't want to rush anything. I've been involved with girls before and
it's, well, you know how it suddenly gets all crazy
and out of control and then you just end up
breaking up and never speaking to each other

again. Well, I don't want that to happen to us."

I shook my head. "Neither do I."

"So, is it okay to take it slow?"

I laughed. "Of course. In fact, I really respect you for telling me this—and that you've prayed about, well, us. That's pretty cool."

"Do you think you'd like to go out on Saturday night? You know, like a real date?"

I grinned. "Sounds good to me."

"All right. Around seven then?"

"Cool."

So I'll be having my first official date this week. My parents told me a couple years ago that I wasn't allowed to date until I turned sixteen. At the time I thought that it was totally unreasonable. But now it actually seems kind of funny, because here I am sixteen and finally going on my first real date. Go figure.

CRAZY HORMONES
You made me
the way You made me
You gave me
this ability to love
like this
please, show me
what to do with
this thing
these feelings

this rush
that's running through me
like a rampaging river
a force of its own
help me
to do things
Your way
amen

Nineteen

Friday, June 27

We had our "business meeting" last night. At first it seemed as though it was going to be smooth sailing—easy breezy. I imagined everyone just signing off on our contract and that would be that. We had invited everyone over to our house, and I even made lemon bars and mint iced tea. To start off with everyone was just happily visiting and acting like it was so great that we'd been offered a contract. We'd already agreed (Allie and Laura and I) that Willy should sort of "chair" the whole thing. So as soon as everyone sat down, he proceeded to give them a pretty thorough explanation of all his concerns with the contract negotiations with Omega.

"I've already had two conversations with Eric," he explained. "And I'm pleased to report that—"

"You've <u>already</u> spoken with Omega?" my mom asked suddenly.

Willy looked slightly taken aback. "Well, that's what we'd all agreed to in Nashville."

My mom glanced at my dad. "I wasn't in Nashville."

Dad nodded toward Willy. "It seemed natural for Willy to handle the negotiations since he's acting as their business manager—"

"I wasn't aware that we'd made that decision final—"

"Mom," I interrupted her. Okay, I was starting to feel pretty ticked with my mother just now. "Allie and Laura and I all agreed even before we went to Nashville that we want Willy for our manager."

"Yes," Dad backed me. "He seems the natural choice, and he's already been doing—"

"I'd like to hear more of what Chloe's mother has to say," said Mrs. Mitchell, her dark eyes flashing.

"Right." My mom nodded in her direction as if they had some secret alliance (and maybe they did). "I'm just worried that things are moving too fast right now."

"Too fast?" Willy stood and cleared his throat. "Well, maybe you don't quite understand the nature of the music industry, but fast is just the way they work. Two weeks to negotiate a contract could be a dangerous thing in some circumstances. Another girl band could come on the scene and turn the heads at Omega, and that's it—" he clapped his hands for emphasis—"Redemption is out on its ear."

I saw Allie's eyes grow wide.

"Yes," my dad picked it up from there. "As it is, considering the holiday ahead, we actually have just a few days to figure this out and get it nailed down. So let's not waste precious time arguing—"

"I thought we were here to ask questions," continued Mrs. Mitchell. "I know I have a few."

"Honey." Mr. Mitchell patted her arm. "Let's give them a chance to explain everything first."

"So anyway," continued Willy, "Omega seems very willing to meet us halfway on just about every—"

"But what about our attorney?" my mom demanded. And she's always telling me not to interrupt. I guess working at a law firm makes some people forget their manners occasionally.

"I thought you were planning to give us a report on your findings," Willy said evenly. I like that this guy doesn't get easily ticked. Another good reason to have him as our manager. "Are you going to share his interpretation of the contract?"

"Yes, but I thought the attorney was going to do the negotiations."

Willy frowned. "Do you really think it's worth paying him an hourly wage to do something we can easily do for—"

"That's not all," my mom continued. And honestly I felt like digging a big hole, just then, and jumping right in. "Our attorney thinks the girls need an agent to represent them."

"An agent?" Willy scratched his head. "Well, now let's see. An agent will take 15 percent, right off the top, and then you add on the attorney, and—"

"And how much will _you_ take?" my mom locked eyes with Willy.

"I'm only negotiating for 10, which is below the going rate. But I've also gotten Omega to agree to a 50 percent increase in their offer."

"_Fifty_ percent?" My dad suddenly stood and gave Willy a high five. "Good job, Willy!"

"Way to go!" I said from my perch on the hearth, restraining myself from jumping up and down and yelling, "See Mom? Willy does know what he's doing!"

"Right on!" said Allie.

"Sounds like Willy's got a handle on the negotiations." Laura's dad grinned.

"It's not _all_ about money," Laura's mom said quickly. "I'm worried about the girls touring—"

"Now, honey—"

"Don't _honey_ me. You know what happened with Christine." Mrs. Mitchell looked very upset now. I knew that Christine was Laura's older sister, the one who'd gotten involved in drugs.

"It's not fair to hold what Christine did against me," said Laura. Then she turned to the rest of us. "Just because my sister got hooked on crank, my parents are overly protective of me."

The room got uncomfortably silent for a few moments. Then I finally spoke. "Well, we have a similar situation in our family." I glanced over to Dad, desperately hoping he'd help me out here. "But I don't think my parents assume the same thing will happen to me."

Dad sighed. "Our older son has some problems too, but I try not to let that negatively influence how I parent Josh and Chloe. I try to respect that they are their own people. And so far they haven't disappointed me." He smiled now. "If anything they've both made me very proud."

Way to go, Dad!

"That's all well and good," said Elise, speaking up for the first time. "But my situation is different. Allie's my older child and she's only fifteen and—"

"Sheesh, Mom. You make it sound like I'm in kindergarten."

"But you've only been in high school for a year."

"But I really want to do this."

Elise folded her arms across her front, leaned back into the couch, and shook her head. But her face looked so sad that I really started to feel sorry for her. I mean, her marriage had just broken up last year, and she has a handicapped child to cope with, and now her only daughter wants to hit the road. Suddenly I had an idea.

"Hey, doesn't our contract include the expenses for a chaperone?" I reminded everyone.

"And that's another thing," said my mom. "I don't know about the rest of you, but I certainly can't leave my job to go touring with the girls."

"I can't either," said Laura's mom. "And I really believe they need a woman to watch over them—that is IF they actually get to do this crazy thing."

Trying to ignore that last comment, I turned to Allie's mom. "How about you, Elise? You're always saying you hate your job anyway."

She brightened for a moment then frowned. "What about Davie? I can't leave him behind."

"What about him?" I asked. "I know I'd love to have him come along."

"Yeah, so would I," chimed in Laura.

"And I'd miss him terribly if he stayed behind," added Allie.

"He could be like our mascot," I suggested hopefully.

Elise shook her head. "But he can be such a handful sometimes."

"We've got a lot of hands," offered Willy.

She almost smiled now. "But what about—what do the rest of you think?"

"I think it's a great plan," said Dad. Dear old Dad!

"I like the idea of having a parent along," said Mr. Mitchell.

Only my mom and Mrs. Mitchell remained silent.

"That doesn't answer everything," my mom said—determined, it seemed, to keep dragging her heels.

"What else is troubling you?" asked Willy in a gentle voice.

"Legal things, financial things, lots of things..."

Suddenly Laura's mom stood up. "Well, it is still troubling me that these are just kids!" The words seemed to explode from her mouth. She shook her fist at the men. "And I will not see them exploited like this. We cannot send them out there to be exposed to all the wickedness in the world. It's just not right. It's—it's irresponsible."

Suddenly the room went dead silent. Even my mom didn't respond. Finally, Willy spoke up. "You know, I think we should all be taking some time to really pray about this whole thing. In fact, I think now is as good a time as any to begin. I know I've been praying about it myself. I keep asking God to show us His way. But I need to beg your forgiveness tonight. I have been remiss this evening. I should have started this meeting out with prayer."

"That sounds like a wise idea, Willy," said Mr. Mitchell in a calm voice.

So we all bowed our heads. And I'm sure that Elise and even my parents felt just a little uncomfortable then. (Since I don't think they have a prayer life to speak of, and according to Allie, Elise doesn't even have a relationship with God.) But at the moment I really didn't care if they were uncomfortable. Because the fact of the matter was and still is: This is God's business. And it'll never fly if we leave Him out of it.

After we prayed Willy started in again. This time he quickly went over his notes and concerns without interruptions, and then he invited questions and discussion from the rest.

Naturally, my mom was the first to leap in. "Okay, it seems to be established that Willy is going to manage the band. And I can see that it's probably a good thing. He appears to understand the music business better than the rest of us, and it's clear that the girls respect him. But would you still like to hear what the attorney thinks?"

Of course, we all did. And my mom proceeded to read from her notes. And ironically (or not) the attorney's concerns were almost identical to Willy's. My dad pointed this out and Mr. Mitchell agreed.

"Now that you mention it—" my mom set her notes on the coffee table and sat down—"I guess you're right." She turned to Willy. "Looks like you're doing a pretty good job."

"Why, thank you." He smiled at her.

"But what about this touring business?" asked Mrs. Mitchell. "I can't bear to have Laura gone for six whole months."

"Mom—"

"Oh, that." Willy waved his hand. "It's not six months in sequence. It's just six months in general. The trips will probably be broken up into a few weeks here and a few weeks there, or perhaps one month on the road and one at home. And Eric even said the girls might not need to tour for the entire six months anyway. Omega just likes to cover themselves legally in case the band becomes really popular and that should happen."

"And I assume that the more concerts they perform, the more money they make?" This from Laura's dad.

"You bet. Everything is based on percentages. How many CDs they sell, how many tickets they sell—the girls will always get their cut."

Mr. Mitchell looked relieved. "I don't know about you people, but I don't mind seeing Laura all set for her college and whatever else comes along. It's an amazing opportunity for all of them."

Elise nodded. "I have to agree with you on that. There's no way I could pay for Allie to go to college with my job as a grocery clerk."

"And I do like the idea of Allie's mother going with the girls," said Mrs. Mitchell, as if she were finally climbing aboard. "I feel much better knowing a parent will be along." She glanced at Willy. "No offense."

"None taken." He smiled. "And if it makes you feel any better, I'll be driving my own little motor home along. It's not nearly as ritzy as what the ladies will have, but it's fine for an old bachelor like me."

"So are we getting close to an agreement here?" asked Willy.

I silently prayed that God would do a miracle.

"It looks like we're closing in on one," said Dad. "Should we put this thing to a vote yet?"

They kicked it around for a few more minutes, then Willy asked everyone to vote. Thank God, it was unanimous. All the parents had come completely around. It really did seem like a miracle after hearing them bicker and argue there for a while. Laura and Allie and I sneaked out and discussed this in the backyard.

"Whew," said Allie. "I thought we were going to get the ax tonight."

"I thought my mom was going to ruin everything," I confessed.

"Or my mom." Laura shook her head. "I didn't realize how badly I wanted this thing until it started to look as if it was caving in."

"It's going to happen," I told them, the excitement creeping back into my voice.

"This is so cool!" Allie's eyes were bright. "I don't think I've ever been this happy before—not in my entire life!"

And I know how she feels. It's like things appeared to be going sideways there for a while, and I almost start to lose hope, then suddenly it all changed, and the next thing you know everything was falling right into place. It makes me believe that God REALLY is guiding this thing. And that makes me more excited than anything.

MAKE US FIT
pieces, so many pieces
how will this puzzle fit?
all sizes, shapes, and colors
come together bit by bit
people, so many people
how will we get along?
so different and so separate
together we'll be strong
mold us, form us, make us
bring us together for You
so we can give You glory
today and our whole lives through
amen

Sunday, June 29

I had a great time with Cesar last night. We didn't do anything really incredible, just burgers and a movie, but it was really fun just being with him.

Cesar came to pick me up at seven. I had tried on about ten different outfits before he arrived. Now, I know this sounds crazy when my "uniform" usually tends to be worn and torn T-shirts and old baggy jeans. You might be wondering: How hard is that? But I really wanted to look special tonight. So I pulled out a couple of the things I'd gotten while shopping with Beanie last week. (We've officially signed her up as our fashion coordinator—it's actually written into the contract.) Anyway, she'd talked me into a couple of things that at first seemed very un-Chloe-like. But somehow she convinced me and I bought them. So finally I decided on this one top with embroidery and a pair of flare jeans. I guess it looked pretty cool. Cesar commented on how nice I looked. It was kind of fun to dress differently.

I must admit that I felt nervous. Why is that? I guess it's because it was a real "date" and it's official now—we are going out. But I was so relieved when Cesar didn't suddenly get all mushy and physical on me. The only thing he did was hold my hand during the movies. And that was just so cool. I really appreciate that about him.

It feels like he really respects me.

Now I suppose I thought he might try a good-night kiss at the door. But instead, he took my hand in his again and just told me how much he'd enjoyed the evening, and then he said good night.

I felt a weird mixture of disappointment and relief. But after thinking about it more carefully, I am glad he did it like that. And I'm even planning on telling Caitlin about it. It might help her to see that it's possible to date without going all hot and crazy.

But here's what's strange about going out and not kissing—it makes everything seem way more romantic. Kind of like those old movies where they don't show too much, but it feels like so much more. It's hard to describe, but I like it.

HONOR
i will honor
myself
my belief
my boyfriend
my parents
but most of all
my God
i want to honor
You
in all i do
and when i do

i know
it will honor
everyone around me
help me to
honor You
amen

Twenty

Friday, July 4

My dad invited everyone connected to the band (as well as anyone else who we wanted to come) to go out to the lake for a day of celebration, picnicking, and boating. Both Dad and his buddy Ron Stephensen had ski boats there and gave kids turns tearing up the lake.

After I'd heard Allie and Laura announce that they were inviting Ryan and Taylor, I felt it only fair to invite Cesar. And of course we asked Caitlin and Beanie to come, and Caitlin brought along her little brother, Benjamin. Altogether I think there must've been more than thirty of us there. It was so cool!

We stayed until late, enjoying the fireworks reflecting off the glass surface of the lake. Very beautiful. Cesar held my hand but did nothing else. And I was perfectly happy with that. I noticed Ryan with his arm around Laura, and even him sneaking a kiss or two when they thought no one was watching. I also noticed Allie and Taylor slip away. And this bothered me. But then I thought, well, her mom and little brother are here—as well as the rest of us. I guess I don't need to worry about her so much. And like she says, she's "not a baby." Besides, it seems as if Taylor is nicer than I thought. Maybe I did misjudge him. I hope so.

SPECTACULAR DISPLAY
Your love
is brighter than fireworks
o my God
Your joy
is more spectacular than a shooting star
Your peace
is more beautiful than the lake in moonlight
Your grace
more refreshing than cool water on a hot day
nothing compares to You
o my God
praise and thanks
I give to You
my God
amen

Saturday, July 5

Willy called this morning and said that Omega has agreed, with a couple of minor changes, to the contract that we FedExed to them after our final vote. I called and left messages for Laura and Allie, and then, too excited to just sit around, I went over to the Paradiso to tell Allie in person. But she wasn't there.

"Where's Al?" I asked Mike. "I thought she worked this morning."

He shrugged. "I thought she did too."

"Maybe she's on her way," I suggested. "I know she's not at home." Then I noticed several customers waiting for their coffees. "You want a hand back there?"

He grinned. "You kidding?"

So I grabbed an apron and started making coffees, thinking that Al would show up at any moment. But by noon, she still hadn't come. And she hadn't answered her phone. "We're supposed to practice at one," I told Mike as I hung up my apron.

He nodded. "Thanks for helping. I owe you bigtime."

I waved my hand. "Hey, you're the one who gave me my first big break in music. I think I owe you."

He laughed, then turned to the next customer.

Laura was just parking her car in front of my house when I got home. "I heard the news," she called as she walked over. "I am so glad that part is over with. I kept thinking my mom was going to change her mind and call the whole thing off."

"Yeah, me too." I parked my bike. "Have you heard from Al today?"

"No, I've been at work."

"She was supposed to have been at work too, but she never showed. And she's not at home."

"Do you think something's wrong?"

I shrugged. "I don't know. Do you suppose something could've happened with Davie?"

"Maybe we should try calling again."

So I went inside and called Allie's number and to my surprise she actually answered. At least I thought it was her, but her voice sounded strange. "Allie?"

"Yeah."

"Are you okay?"

She didn't answer, just made a sniffling sound.

"Are you crying?"

Again she didn't answer, but I could tell she was crying.

"What's wrong, Al?"

"Noth—nothing."

"It doesn't sound like nothing. Are you okay?"

"Yeah, I guess so."

"What happened? Is it your mom? Davie?"

"They're okay."

"Then _what_?" I was losing my patience, and Laura looked as if the suspense was killing her.

"I said it's nothing."

"Allie, why didn't you go to work this morning?"

"I—uh—I forgot."

"Yeah." I made a face to Laura to show her I

couldn't make any sense of this either. "So are you coming?"

"Coming?"

"Allie! What is wrong with you? We have practice at one. Willy will be here any minute and—"

"Yeah, I guess I'm coming."

I glanced at Laura. "Do you need a ride?"

"Maybe so."

"Fine. I'll see if Laura can get you." Then I hung up.

"What's going on?" Laura asked.

"I wish I knew. Allie is acting really strange. Can you go pick her up while I wait here for Willy?"

"Sure. I'll be right back."

After Laura left I started to pray. First I prayed for Allie because it seemed like something was seriously wrong. I wondered if she got in a fight with her mom, or maybe her dad called and started acting like a jerk again. But it occurred to me as I prayed that this whole recording contract business was totally dependent on all three of us girls. If one of us falls down, we all fall down. And it got me seriously worried. So I prayed even harder.

When Willy arrived, I told him that something was wrong with Allie. I figured since he's our manager, he might as well get used to stuff like this.

"What is it?" he asked.

"I don't know. She missed work this morning, and when I called just now she sounded really upset. But she wouldn't say. Laura went to get her."

He scratched his head. "That doesn't sound like our Allie."

"Yeah, that's what I was thinking. I was just praying for her."

"Mind if I join you?"

So the two of us took a few more minutes to pray for Al, and the next thing we knew she and Laura were walking in the door.

As soon as I saw her, I knew something really bad must be wrong. Her normally pale face was red and blotchy, like she'd been crying for days without stopping, and her blue eyes were bright and puffy and rimmed in red. She really looked hideous.

I immediately went over and hugged her. "Whatever it is, we will help you through this."

"Do you want to talk about it?" asked Willy in a gentle voice.

She shook her head. "I just want to practice and go home."

"You sure you feel like it?" asked Laura.

She nodded. "Yeah. I can do this."

"Want some iced tea?" I asked.

"That'd be good."

So we got everyone situated with a tall glass of tea, then quietly went upstairs to practice. But it was weird. It's like something was missing, like we were just mechanically running through the steps. And it worried me.

"That's probably good for the day," said Willy after just an hour, his brow furrowed with concern. "I wanted to give you girls an update on what's happening with Omega." He glanced at Allie. "That is, unless you're ready to talk, Al?"

She shook her head and looked down at the drums.

"Okay then." He took in a deep breath, and I could tell this thing with Al was making him pretty nervous. "Omega wants you girls to come back out in a couple weeks to start recording."

"All right!" Laura started to get excited, then turned and looked at Allie as if to see if it was okay.

"Cool," I said. "How long do they expect it will take?"

"It could take up to two weeks."

"Two weeks?" Laura blinked. "Wow."

"And here's what's really exciting," he continued. "After you're done recording, they want you to do some shows."

"Some shows?" I felt a tremor of excitement running through me. "Like <u>real</u> shows, like concerts?"

He smiled. "Well, they won't be big shows, and you're not ready to open for Iron Cross yet. But they've got some advance open bookings at county fairs, spots where they can slot in any of their contracted musicians, and they think it might be a good way to get you girls into real performance shape."

"Hey, it works for me." I glanced over at Allie again. "What do you think, Al?"

She nodded without looking up. "Yeah, cool."

Okay, something in me just exploded about then. I mean, I felt sorry for her and I knew she was really hurting about something, but it's pretty aggravating when someone won't even tell you what's going on. "What is wrong with you?" I actually shouted.

She looked at me, then burst into tears.

"I'm sorry," I muttered as I went over and stood by her. "I'm really sorry, Allie. But can't you see it's really frustrating? I mean, we're all excited about what's going on—and here you are totally falling apart on us. You have to tell us what's wrong, Al. We're a team—a family. It's just not fair to keep something from us."

She looked over to where Willy and Laura were silently watching us both. "I'm—I'm sorry, you guys. I'm just such a—such a mess today." Allie frowned at me. "I know you're right, Chloe. But it's hard to—"

"Would it be easier to tell just one of us, Allie?" asked Willy. "It's plain to see you need to talk to someone."

She nodded, then pointed at me. "I—I'll tell Chloe." She wiped her wet face with her hands. "Before she beats it out of me."

I kind of smiled then turned to Willy and Laura. "We'll all talk later." And they left. Laura didn't even take her bass with her. I'm sure they were both pretty freaked by this whole thing. I know I was. I also knew they'd both be praying for Allie—and me too.

I flopped down on the couch and waited a few minutes, hoping this might help her to recover. Finally, she climbed down from her stool and came over and sank down beside me. She reached for a throw pillow and clutched it to herself and started to speak.

"It's about Taylor."

I waited for her to continue, but when she didn't, I asked her, "Did he break up with you?"

She turned and looked at me with angry eyes. "No!"

"Okay." I leaned back and exhaled loudly. "What then?"

"I broke up with him."

I brightened now. "What's wrong with that?"

She shook her head. "You just don't get it."

"Duh. I'm not a mind reader, you know."

"Last night..."

"Yeah, I saw you guys sneaking away last night. What happened?" But it's as if she didn't need to tell me. Maybe I was a mind reader after all, because somehow I thought I knew.

"We went for a walk." Then she started to cry again.

I sat up and peered into her face. "Allie? Did Taylor do something to you? Did he force you to—"

She shook her head. "He didn't—didn't actually rape me, Chloe. Really, he didn't."

"Okay," I tried to speak soothingly. "Did he try to rape you?"

She nodded, silent tears now streaming down her cheeks. Then we both just sat there for a few minutes. I was stunned, yes, but not completely surprised. It seemed like the kind of thing that Taylor Russell would do. And for the first time since my encounters with Tiffany Knight, I really wanted to do some bodily harm to someone. I know we're supposed to let God take revenge, but at that moment I wouldn't have minded being able to dish out a little of my own.

"I really thought he loved me," she finally said, breaking through the wall of silence.

"Yeah, I know you did, Al."

"He said I was special."

"He's a liar, Al. According to Cesar, Taylor

Russell is after one thing and one thing only."

"I thought he was so cool." She pulled out the hem of her T-shirt and wiped her nose on it. "I thought I was pretty cool too—having Taylor Russell interested in me. It was like a fairy tale."

"With a really rotten ending."

"Yeah." Then she proceeded to tell me how he'd led her to an isolated area and began kissing her. "It wasn't the first time we'd kissed," she admitted. "And Taylor was always kind of pressing me for more, but usually we were around other people, or I'd make some excuse about curfew or whatever. I just figured he was acting like a normal guy, you know?"

"Not all guys are like that." I thought of Cesar.

She shook her head. "I feel so stupid for falling for him. You tried to warn me, Chloe." Then she told me how he'd held her by her arms, even after she begged him to let go, how he pinned her down on the ground. "There was a sharp stick under me." She pulled up the back of her shirt to show a big red gash on her back. "And I kept saying no, but the fireworks were so loud."

"I'm so sorry, Al." I put my hand on her shoulder. "I was worried about you—when I saw you guys leave. I should've come."

"You didn't know..." She rolled her eyes. "I

didn't even know. Even when it was happening, I thought, 'This cannot be happening to me.' But he was pulling on my shirt and my shorts and no matter what I said to him, he just kept going." She stopped to take in a jagged breath.

"But you said he didn't—"

"I just started praying, Chloe. I don't even know if I was praying out loud or in my head, but I started begging God to help me. And the whole time I was trying to kick and punch. Then suddenly Taylor looked up, like I think he heard someone walking toward us. I never actually heard or saw anyone myself. But Taylor jumped up, zipped his jeans, and just took off running. I never saw him again last night." Now she really started sobbing. "And—and—he just left me there—like this broken toy—or something he didn't need anymore. I felt so—so—" She put her head into the pillow and cried.

"Used," I finished for her.

Allie spent the night at my house tonight. Apparently she was in such shock the evening it all happened, that although her mom drove her and Davie home from the lake, she didn't even cry or speak or anything. And she hasn't told her mom about any of this, and she's afraid to now.

I told her that I think she should: 1) tell her mom, and 2) tell the police. But Allie refused. She's afraid it will ruin everything for us—that somehow her mom will think it has to do with the band. Or that Laura's mom, or even mine, will. And while I can sort of see her point, I still think she needs to tell her story. It's wrong for someone like Taylor Russell to just walk around doing <u>that</u> to girls. I told Allie that I wouldn't bug her about it anymore tonight, if she promised to really consider the bigger picture tomorrow. She said she would if I promised not to tell anyone.

"Not even Laura?" I asked.

"<u>No one.</u>"

So now I'm really torn. Is it right to keep something like this a secret? But if I can't tell anyone, who do I go to for advice? I guess the place to start is with God.

WHAT TO DO
what to do
i know that You know
what is right
what is good
what is best
o God
i don't have a clue
i feel confused
please, show me
show us both
what to do

with this
injustice
show us
Your way
amen

Twenty-one

Monday, July 14

Okay, I realize that you can't force anyone to do something against her will—well, not without breaking the law (like Taylor Russell has done). And I know after eight long days of begging and pleading and even threatening that Allie is <u>not</u> going to tell her mother. Just as she is <u>not</u> going to go to the police and report Taylor's attempted rape. At first I was really upset by this. It feels so wrong to me. I even asked Allie if she's sure that she's doing what God wants her to do. "What if you're disobeying God?" I asked her as we drove home from church yesterday.

"Believe me, I've prayed about this, Chloe. I really have. And this is what comes to me. First off, it's partly my fault—"

"Oh, Allie!"

"Just hear me out. I'm not saying it IS my fault. I don't go in for that blame-the-girl crud. But I am saying that I allowed myself to be in the wrong place at the wrong time with the wrong person."

I nodded. "Okay, that makes sense. But just the

same, it really is Taylor's fault for acting like such a jerk-face."

"Duh. Tell me something I don't know. But the thing is, I had a choice in the matter, and I made a bad choice. I think I need to learn something from it."

"But why don't you think God wants you to tell your mom?"

"What good would that do her right now?"

"I don't know."

"Honestly, I think she has enough on her hands with my dad and this babysitter lady who's not taking very good care of Davie. I mean, there's absolutely nothing she can do about this whole thing—other than to worry and feel bad. Why should I put her through that?"

I shrugged.

Then she poked me in the arm. "Well, what about you? Would you tell _your_ parents if it had happened to you?"

I had to think about that. I never even considered telling them about the jerk in middle school who pressured me for sex, then ruined my life with lies. But maybe I should've. "I don't know, Allie."

"Some things aren't just plain black and white."

"Maybe not. But what about Taylor? How come he gets off free as a bird?"

"Yeah, that's what bugs me."

"Well, it bugs me too. I know that God doesn't want us to take our own revenge." I kind of laughed. "Not that I don't have a few ideas."

"Yeah, me too."

"But it seems wrong that Taylor is free to walk the streets and possibly do it again. Maybe even succeed next time."

"Yeah. I feel bad about that too."

"But not bad enough to go to the police?"

"It's like I've already said, Chloe, he didn't actually rape me. I don't have any evidence. It would be his word against mine. And what good would it really do? You know what they put girls through who make charges like that? I saw this TV movie once, and it was really awful—and she'd actually been raped. I'm just not sure I'd want to go through all that."

I nodded. "Yeah, to be honest, I guess I wouldn't either. But there should be some way to warn others about Taylor."

"Yeah, like maybe take out an ad in the paper."

I laughed. "Yeah, a full page one with his photo on it, saying: Beware of dangerous rapist, Taylor Russell. He may look good and say all the right things, but he's a big fat phony."

She laughed. "Yeah, something like that."

"Or maybe we could do a billboard, that enormous one right next to the freeway entrance with all the spotlights."

"Bet that'd cost a fortune. If it wasn't illegal I could do some graffiti on the side of the school, make it really artistic, you know? Just a gentle warning to all the girls at Harrison High. No big deal."

I laughed. "Yeah, then you'd be locked up for vandalism and Taylor would still be on the prowl."

"But maybe the girls would be more careful with guys like him." Allie sighed. "Honestly, I wish there was a way to tell people without actually going around and saying it."

"He'd probably sue you for slander if you did. His dad's a lawyer, you know."

"It figures. I just wish we could do something anonymous, Chloe."

"Like what?"

"Not something just to be mean. I really don't believe God wants me to do something out of revenge. But I guess I do feel responsible to warn other girls like me."

"Yeah, it makes me wonder if he's gotten away with it before."

"Hey, what if I wrote an anonymous letter and sent it to a bunch of girls at school and asked them to get the word around?"

I thought about it. "You know, that might actually work."

So we went to my house and carefully constructed a short letter to warn girls about the dangers of dating Taylor Russell and other boys like him. Allie dictated and I typed. We revised it several times to keep it brief and to the point. No sense in getting melodramatic.

"It's kind of like how the apostles wrote letters," I said as we printed the copies out. "I mean, what we're saying here is completely true and for the girls' own good if they take it to heart."

"Yeah." Allie smiled as she continued making the list of girls to send the letter to. "It feels so much better knowing that I'm doing something to prevent this from happening again."

Then we got out the phone book, and while Allie read the addresses aloud, I typed them into my computer's label format program. After everything was printed out, we deleted all the original files—just in case Taylor's dad tried to trace this back to us someday, which seemed highly unlikely, but added to the suspense.

"That's the first time I've been thankful that I don't have a PC," said Allie, laughing. "Taylor won't be able to accuse me of doing this."

"I feel like we should be in a spy movie."

Then I borrowed my mom's car and we drove over to the next town (part of our undercover routine), bought a box of legal-sized envelopes, then went back to the car and stuffed them and put labels on. Then we went to the post office and bought stamps from the machine (no witnesses), stamped the envelopes, and put them in the slot. We thought it was covertly clever to have them mailed from another town. Then we went home in time to get ready for practice.

Willy and Laura both seem relieved that things are returning to normal now. Willy's got us practicing every day again until we go to Nashville. And Allie used "breaking up with Taylor" as her excuse for falling apart the other day, and it seemed to satisfy both of them. But I expect the word will be getting around (to Laura and everyone else) that Taylor is a jerk, although we didn't send Laura a letter. We felt pretty certain that she was too smart to go out with a creep like Taylor. Besides, she's still smitten with Ryan anyway.

So even though Allie didn't handle things the way I thought she should (at least initially), I think what she did was right—for her. It was really her choice, and who am I to question what she believes God is saying to her? She did assure me, however, that she does plan to tell her mom about the whole thing—someday, when the timing seems right. I've got to respect her for that.

CONFUSION
crazy days
hazy ways

upside-down
and inside out
what is right
not always clear
God's the One
we need to hear
cm

Monday, July 21

We're on our way to Nashville again. This time
with Willy and Elise as our chaperones, and little
Davie along for the ride. It's kind of weird, but I
feel older this time, more mature somehow. And
Allie and Laura seem older to me too. How is this
possible in only one month's time?

Maybe it's because we know what to expect now.
Or maybe our confidence level has increased as a
result of the legal contract that proclaims in
bold black and white that we are now "professional musicians." And yet, at the same time, I
think I might need to pinch myself—to see if this
is all really real.

But just as I'm questioning reality, little
Davie comes down the aisle and pours a whole bag
of peanuts right into my lap, and I remember that,
yes, this is real.

Cesar came over to my house last night, and we
sat and talked about everything for a long time.

We've decided that we're going to keep in touch through letters—yes, old-fashioned hand-written letters. It was his idea since I didn't think I'd have much access to a computer to do e-mail. But I think it's a lovely idea. And I already started writing him one during this flight. Allie made fun of me when she saw what I was doing. But then she apologized and said it was probably just because she was jealous.

"I wish I'd had the sense to pick out a better boyfriend," she whispered (since her mom was sitting right in front of us).

"Hey, at least you learned something from it," I reminded her.

She smiled. "Actually, I've been thinking about what Caitlin said to our youth group last week."

"You mean about not dating?" I still wasn't sure what I thought about this whole abstaining from dating thing. I mean, it's one thing to abstain from sex—and I'm for sure doing that—but the dating thing still isn't too clear to me. I'm asking God to show me what's best for me. But from where I'm sitting, I honestly don't see anything wrong with my relationship with Cesar. Believe it or not, we haven't even kissed yet.

Allie nodded. "I really gave some serious thought to her challenge. In fact, I called her up a couple days ago, and we had this nice long talk about the whole thing."

"Did you tell her about Taylor?"

"Not in so many words, but I hinted at a bad relationship."

"So are you going to become like Caitlin?" I could hear the teasing tone in my voice, and instantly regretted it. "Not that it would be so bad. Caitlin is pretty cool."

"Well, I'm praying about it." She leaned back and sighed. "And to be honest, it sounds like a smart way to go right now. Especially since I've already shown that I'm not the best judge of character—especially when it comes to really cute guys." She giggled. "You know, like Jeremy Baxter..."

"Oh, no." I groaned. "Don't tell me you're getting a crush on the lead guitar player of Iron Cross. You haven't even met him."

"I know. But he is so cute."

Here we go again, I'm thinking. "Well, maybe you're right."

"Huh?"

"Maybe you should consider Caitlin's challenge."

She playfully punched me in the arm, but I think she knows I only have her best interests at heart. And it hurt me a lot to witness her pain all because of a stupid, selfish, totally depraved boy. I just don't want to see her going through anything like that ever again.

Especially when I think of everything that God has in store for us—why would we want to do anything to jeopardize this great ride? When I consider the doors He's kicking open for us, the amazing journey He's taking us on, and how He might use our music to touch lives...Well, why take chances with that?

WINGS BENEATH ME
i can fly
in God's arms
i sail so high
high above those
earthly things
in God's love
i have wings
cm

Twenty-two

Monday, August 11

It was a long, grueling two weeks in Nashville. We thought we'd never get done. I guess we should be grateful that we had absolutely no idea (well, maybe Willy did) how much harder it is to do a professional recording than the simple little demo we did last spring. Long hours, working late into the night, countless retakes—it was like a music marathon.

We came prepared with about thirty songs we felt pretty comfortable with, and the powers that be then selected their top fifteen favorites just based on the lyrics alone. At first, I wasn't too pleased with some of the songs that were cut, but Willy explained that it had to do with balancing the album, and I realized that we'd have to trust them on this.

Naturally, all the songs were written by me and arranged by Willy, well, along with a little help from the producers and mixers. Everybody's an expert. Actually, the suggestions we received were mostly pretty helpful. One morning they tried to do a photo shoot while we were recording. Talk about a circus! But somehow it all worked out.

The editing and mixing should be finished by
now, and according to Willy, the CD is being fast-
track produced and we may even have copies by
the end of the month. Omega is really breaking
the speed barriers on this one. Willy said it has
more to do with Iron Cross than us—since they're
in dire need of a warm-up band. But even that
remains to be seen. Eric Green said that if we
don't make the grade on the road, it'll all be for
nothing. High stakes. Still, he assured us, "You
girls have the right stuff." I hope he's right.

Anyway, we were so thankful to be done. After
we got home, Laura slept for two whole days, and
Allie said she doesn't care if we ever make
another CD—ever! Elise said she thought it was
like giving birth—you'd forget about the pain
when the time came to do it all over again. I'm not
really sure what she means since I've never had a
baby, but I hope she's right about forgetting
about it.

We got to enjoy a few brief and blissful days at
home, and then it was time to hit the road again
for our very first concert tour. Family and
friends gathered in front of our church, where
our tour motor coach was parked, to tell us good-
bye.

But before we got on the RV, Willy gave us a
sweet little speech. "I know I'm not your dad," he
began, "but I guess I think of you girls as the

closest thing to my very own daughters. So you can count on me to act as protective as a real dad, maybe even more so." He glanced toward our families and grinned. "And you know I've promised your parents that I'll do my best to keep you girls in line."

"That's a big promise, Willy," I teased and the three of us giggled.

He nodded. "I realize that. I also know that going on the road is tough on musicians. It's been the ruin of many." He shook his head sadly. "Including yours truly. But I've learned my lessons the hard way. And you girls are way ahead of the game already. You've got God leading your way. And you've got lots of good people all around you who care about you and believe in you. We're all very proud of you, and we know that you won't do anything to let us down. God bless Redemption!" he shouted, raising his fist in the air.

Our friends and family clapped and cheered at this, then everyone quieted down as Pastor Tony led us all in a prayer. After that we whooped like wild things as we boarded our big shiny RV, waving and blowing kisses to the small crowd of onlookers like we thought we were real celebrities—which we do not.

Eric was right on about our touring accommodations. _Very nice_. It looked like a great big

Greyhound bus on the outside, only nicer, but had all the comforts of home on the inside—TV, VCR, CD player, microwave, full kitchen, fairly roomy bathroom, comfortable beds and seating—the works! Oh, I suppose it could feel cramped in here after a few months, but right now it feels as though we're just taking off for some really great vacation.

The driver is a large African-American woman named Rosy. At first she seemed a little gruff and almost scary, but now I can see it's just a surface thing. Underneath it she's got this really tender heart. I know this because I sat up with her talking until pretty late last night while the others were asleep. She told me about how she'd been married to a real jerk who used to "knock her around after he'd been drinking." They had a little girl named Violet, but then the girl got sick and died, and Rosy decided to just "up and leave the jerk behind."

She borrowed enough money to put herself through truck driving school—and now here she is. She's also a Christian and doesn't mind sharing her faith with anyone she meets along the way.

I told her I'm glad that she's our driver and I hope that we don't make her too crazy with our music and noise and general goofiness. She laughed and said, "I just pretend that my Violet's along with us. She would be about your age by now. I think she'd enjoy the ride."

I think she would too. Our schedule looks fairly busy with a lot of road in between stops, but Rosy makes good time on the highway. During the day, we practice, play games, and watch videos, as well as chase after Davie. So far so good, but it's only been two days.

Our first real concert is tomorrow. "Just a county fair," Willy said. But hey, it's the big times to us, and we'll play for the fair goers no differently than if we were performing at Madison Square Garden in front of thousands.

We've all agreed that whatever we do with our music, we are going to do it all out for God. No holding back. Even if only three people show up to watch us tomorrow, we'll give them their money's worth. And if they got in for free, we'll play even harder.

Oh, I know it might be tough to maintain these high standards, but I believe God will help us to do our best. And maybe in time, our concerts will all be "sold out." It could happen. Who knows?

In the meantime, I know that I am totally "sold out." Sold out on God, that is!

SOLD OUT!
sold out
don't hold out

all i am
all i have
all i do
belongs to You
sold out
don't hold out
mercy
grace
Your love
from above
sold out
on You
amen

The publisher and author would love to hear your
comments about this book. *Please contact us at:*
www.multnomah.net/diary

Discussion Questions

1. Chloe was hurt when Pastor Rawlins said her music "didn't have God in it." How do you feel about the way she handled this when she met with him?

2. At one point, it feels as if the band Redemption is finished. How does this impact Chloe's faith?

3. After experiencing Marissa's shoplifting episode once, do you think Chloe and Allie should've gone to the mall with her a second time? Have you ever experienced a situation like this? If so, how did you handle it?

4. Chloe is a real dreamer. What does she do that helps her dreams become reality?

5. Chloe cares deeply for kids with problems. Do you think it's smart for her to hang with friends who aren't following God?

6. After Allie is nearly raped by her "boyfriend," Chloe wants her to go to the police, but Allie refuses. What would you do if you were Allie's friend?

7. Chloe is very creative. Why do you think that is? Do you have room for more creativity in your life?

8. When Redemption starts becoming known, some of Chloe's previous enemies want to become friends. How would you handle "friends" like that?

9. Unlike Caitlin, Chloe doesn't feel that God has told her <u>not</u> to date. Do you think she's making a mistake by getting involved with Cesar?

10. Chloe's highest purpose in life is to be "sold out" on God. What is yours?

THE DIARY OF A TEENAGE GIRL SERIES
UNLOCKS THE SECRETS OF GROWING UP!

HEY, GOD, WHAT DO YOU WANT FROM ME?

More and more teens find themselves growing up in a world lacking in godly wisdom and direction. In *Piercing Proverbs,* bestselling youth fiction author Melody Carlson offers solid messages of the Bible in a version that can compete with TV, movies, and the Internet for the attention of this vital group in God's kingdom. Choosing life-impacting portions of teen-applicable Proverbs, Carlson paraphrases them into understandable, teen-friendly language and presents them as guidelines for clearly identified areas of life (such as friendship, family, money, and mistakes). Teens will easily read and digest these high-impact passages of the Bible delivered in their own words.

ISBN 1-57673-895-7

www.letstalkfiction.com

Let's Talk Fiction is a free, four-color minimagazine created to give readers a "behind the scenes" look at Multnomah Publishers' favorite fiction authors. ***Let's Talk Fiction*** allows our authors to share a bit about themselves, giving readers an inside peek into their latest releases. Published in the fall, spring, and summer seasons, ***Let's Talk Fiction*** is filled with interactive contests, author contact information, and fun! To receive your free copy of ***Let's Talk Fiction***, get on-line at www.letstalkfiction.com. We'd love to hear from you!